SOUL OF THORNS

WICKED FAE

STACEY TROMBLEY

SOUL of THORNS

WICKED FAE

BOOK 3

STACEY TROMBLEY

1
CAELYNN

I push harder, feet thumping over the uneven ashy terrain. Dark fluid flutters from the sky like flurries of snow, except instead of the gentle sting of frost, it's the harsh bite of acid. The searing pain scatters over every inch of exposed skin, leaving red welts behind, but I clench my jaw and push through the pain.

We're getting closer to the center of the Schorchedlands. The air is thick in my lungs. Sweat drips down my back and beads on my forehead as the heat presses in. The poison in the atmosphere gets stronger until it feels like the acid isn't only on my skin—it's inside me. Will I even know it when I reach the inner circle, where a mortal cannot survive even an hour? Will I realize the life is being sucked from my body before it's too late?

Every lung full sends more pain cascading through my chest but I don't dare focus on that now.

Now, he is in trouble. Now, I might lose him. And I cannot let that happen.

That's all there is now—pain and determination. I run because I must. I try to use the pain to my advantage, to become *the pain. But it weighs on me. Heavier and heavier, tearing at the light inside of me, dying like a soft ember barely clinging to hope.*

"If he dies, you'll be free to escape," a familiar voice purrs in my ear, even as I sprint over the rubble of this broken place. Scarred and toxic, just like my own soul.

"No," I growl through my painful breaths.

My wraith floats effortlessly beside me. Frustration fills me at as his ease, his calm. It sends a wave of fury over my body, and I fight against a roar of anger. That will not help me now.

That won't help Rev.

Instead, I use the anger as more fuel. I will prove the wraith wrong. I will become one with the shadows. Angry magic rushes through my veins, pulsing with every movement. It hisses in my ear and presses in on my vision until all I see is darkness.

I can use the magic within the natural element of shadows to my advantage, and here, it is everywhere. In everything.

Except here, it is not my friend. Here, the darkness wishes to devour my very soul. It claws deeper and deeper every moment I use it. Not unlike the Night Bringer so long ago. How his magic carved through my body like butter and left a seared edge and shattered soul behind. Even Rev with his healing magic can't save me from those wounds.

But I can still save him.

The way he looks at me now... I wince and push the image away. Because it isn't real. It isn't possible. He couldn't possibly adore me the way his expression last night implied. And if he does... he'll regret it soon enough.

Because I destroy everything I love.

"I belong here, you fool," I tell the wraith. "One day, you'll accept that."

"If you stay," the wraith whispers, "the Night Bringer will take away more of you, piece by piece, until it's only his magic that remains. Then, he will free himself with ease. It will be his soul inside your body, reigning over the Shadow Court. On that day, Caelynn, Princess of the Shadow Court, you'll lose everything you ever dared to hope for."

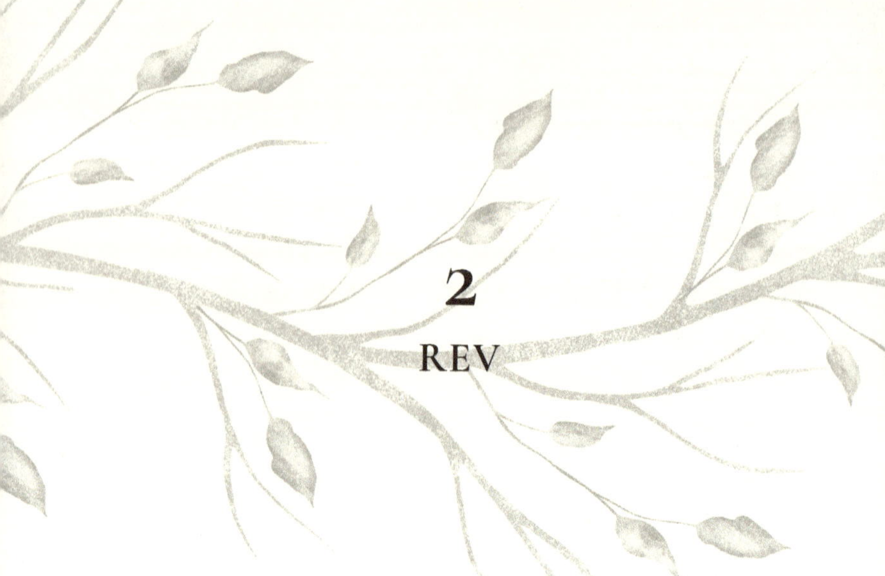

2
REV

I take in a long breath, watching the shadows shift over the dark waters. The dull, hazy light of the sun is just rising over the horizon behind a film of fog. The shift is subtle. Our surroundings grow progressively lighter as the night ends and day begins, but in this place, that only means a haze of reddish light over dark lands. It's enough to keep the wraiths hidden—mostly—but not enough to make this hellish landscape bright or friendly.

The mumbling voices of the dead can occasionally be heard in the hills surrounding our little valley. Their smoke magic wafts to and fro on the rocky hillsides.

Is one of them my brother? I wonder as I sit on a rock and watch the bubbling tar-like waters of the swamp where I last saw him. Where I threw him into the oily pit and watched him flee.

I fought my brother for Caelynn.

It's still hard to wrap my mind around, to be honest.

The brother I've hero-worshiped since I was a child. The brother I'd vowed to avenge against the female sleeping soundly in the cottage behind me. The female I'm now determined to protect.

I twist a little white stone between my fingers, watching the reddish light reflect off of it.

When I grabbed the stone from my court, I hadn't thought it would mean much. A symbol of what I'd lost. But as time goes on, it means more and more.

We have a home here, a little hand-built, rickety cottage that's covered in mildew and dust and protected by magic. We have enough supplies to survive temporarily... but not to thrive.

Our first two nights here, I stayed awake until early morning, keeping watch as Caelynn slept. While wraiths groaned in the distance. But they never came near.

It didn't take long for my guard to fall and for my attention to turn away from the anticipation of a fight to watching Caelynn's pained expression as she tossed and turned on the uneven straw bed.

The wound my brother gave her was significant. I've never feared death more than I feared hers. Another question to add to my list. I've felt so many conflicting things about the lovely shadow fae. I've hated her. I've desired her death. I've respected her. I've grown to care for her, even as I distrusted her. I felt betrayed by her— only to learn that once again, she was sacrificing to help me.

I don't think I'll ever know everything she's done for me.

And all I've ever done is hurt her.

Now, it might be too late to change that. By entering the Schorchedlands, she made her biggest sacrifice yet.

Only one of us can leave this place, and I know she intends for it to be me.

The hair on my arms stands up suddenly, and the air around me cools. My gaze flashes to the inky-black waters of the swamp then up to a dark form hovering over it only a few feet away.

The breath catches in my throat. The wraith wafts gently. Silently. His smoke-like form swirls and shifts, but the hole where his eyes should be is black. Empty of emotion. No aggression or anger or fear—nothing.

Muscles tense, scarcely breathing, I slowly rise from my seat on the uneven stone, eyes never leaving the wraith.

I've seen dozens of wraiths over the last few days but only from afar. Their voices carry over the mountain range as they roam randomly, but they leave this valley mostly alone. Since I fought Reahgan, since he failed to kill Caelynn in order to "save me," they've kept their distance. They've never come within a hundred feet of either of us.

Light flickers in my palm, ready to fight. I could kill him easily, quickly, but the use of my magic would draw more wraiths to us. So, instead, I wait.

The wraith doesn't draw closer. It doesn't speak. In fact, it's only movement is gentle swaying as he hovers over the swamp.

Then, a cry of pain grabs my attention. My blood turns to ice as I whip my head toward the cottage. *Caelynn.*

The terror of her voice causes my gut to clench, and without another moment of hesitation, I sprint back to our temporary home. Panic rushes over my body as I pound over the ashen ground and shove through the crooked wooden door. "Caelynn?" I call.

In only an instant, I size up the room. The wards are still intact, and the cottage is quiet. No evidence of wraiths or other creatures anywhere nearby.

Caelynn is sitting up in bed, blond hair falling into her face as she pants desperately, holding her throat. I rush to her, a knee on the bed beside her and a hand braced on the wall as I lean over her, prepared to heal an injury. "What's wrong?" I croak, placing two fingers under her chin. I lift her face towards mine.

Her expression flickers between confusion and pain and fear.

"I'm fine." Her voice is sharp. Determined.

I swallow as I notice our proximity. Our faces are inches apart. Her eyes flicker to my chest, to my eyes, and then away.

"I'm fine," she says again, pulling her face from my gentle grip.

Slowly, I lean back. I don't have an issue with being... close to her, but she's made it clear over the last few days that she's not comfortable with intimacy. She's been standoffish since we've been here, leaving me wondering if I'd been wrong about everything.

I kissed her in a moment of passion. I'd thought she was going to die. She almost did die. And I acted on my craving. But maybe the desire is one-sided.

Maybe she hasn't forgiven me for believing the worst of her over and over.

Caelynn presses her palms to her eyes.

"What's wrong?" I ask.

"Nothing," she says, rubbing her face rigorously. "Just a dream."

I let out a long breath, working to convince my body I don't need to fight something. It's hard to imagine we've spent three days in the middle of fae hell, with a bounty on our heads but without facing any new wraiths—well, so far. I glance out the one tiny window at the end of the room. The other is boarded shut.

The room is small, just a bed and a "kitchen" with pots, a heath, and a narrow well. There are three crates lining the far wall filled with emptied jars and tin cans. The sorcerer that built this place to study the wraiths had brought a significant amount of supplies but went through almost all of them before his departure.

I stride to the stove and spend a moment building magic in my palm until it grows hot, then I cast a small ray of light onto a chip of glass made to magnify light. In only a moment, there is a spark of flame, and in a few more, the fire is strong enough to heat a pot of water.

"Tea?" I ask her, though I already know the answer.

We only have four servings of tea left, but we hadn't planned on staying much longer.

She nods slowly.

"Want to tell me about it?" I ask casually. Caelynn isn't exactly forthcoming with her emotions, and I don't get the impression she wants to push the boundaries of what we already are. Even just a moment of our eyes connecting causes pain to flicker in her expression.

Caelynn has had enough pain in her life, I don't need to add to it. And since I am not in a position to promise her anything, I haven't pushed her on it. Maybe one day. Maybe I'll figure out what I feel about the incredibly beautiful shadow fae. Maybe in some faraway future, there is hope for us. It's small, but I refuse to accept that there isn't some way we could each find happiness.

She shakes her head in answer to my offer.

I smirk. Very articulate, this one.

"Hurry with the tea, we should get going," she says as she swings her legs over the edge of the bed, trying to hide a wince.

I roll my eyes. "We don't have to rush out of here. The wraiths haven't bothered us in the slightest and—"

"And you want to wait until they do?" she spits, meeting my eyes for only one quick moment before returning to her mud-caked boots. I suppose it's a good thing I left out my face to face with a wraith moments ago. I glance out the small window again, but there doesn't seem to be any sign of the wraith. Maybe it was a coincidence.

"We agreed we'd leave today," she says. "The faster we complete this quest, the faster we can get you out of here."

I pause, staring at the boiling pot of water.

Me. Get me out of here, not her. She's never, not once implied she would want to leave this place in my stead. Why? Doesn't she want to save herself? Doesn't she hope for something more than this?

Don't you? a voice whispers in my mind. I take in a deep breath. I do want more. I have hope for a grand life. Of power and adoration, of making a difference. Of being remembered. But only one of us can have that chance. And she just freely gives it away without so much as a blink.

One day, I want to give something meaningful back to her. I've taken so much without even realizing it. She shielded me from it all. She let me hate her when she could have come out with the truth and eased her punishment.

I peer out the window. We're several miles into the Schorchedlands by now. I can't even see the thorn walls that border these lands. All I can see are the rocky hills surrounding us and the dull sky, but even so, I know there's a whole world out there waiting for us. For me. My eyes drift back to Caelynn busy buttoning her jacket.

She'll willingly leave all hope behind for me, but that's all the more reason to fight for her.

3
CAELYNN

Hazy light streams through the last intact window of the shadow-filled cottage, casting a reddish glow over Rev. I watch his movements, his muscles shifting as he pours water over the pot, measuring a small amount of tea into the filter and placing it in carefully. I watch how he pauses to stare out the window.

What is he thinking about? I wonder.

He's probably annoyed with me for being here. I did complicate things considerably. He's probably thinking about the spell book and how that's the key to his redemption. The key to earning his place as the most powerful fae in the realm.

We've been here for a full three days. Me and Rev, together, in this dinky, hand-built home where soot clings to everything, including us, with meager supplies and very little hope.

Finally, Rev pours the steaming liquid into two small cups, sending pleasant-smelling herbs wafting through the air. I meet his eyes, dull grey. Not nearly as bright as they once were.

Will I ever see their striking color again?

He hands me the ceramic mug, and I grip it with both hands, relishing the warmth.

"Thank you," I grumble awkwardly. He chuckles and sits beside me as he sips his beverage. This will be the last of our quiet moments together. Bittersweet, painful, awkward, and incredibly beautiful.

I close my eyes and focus on the warmth, of his drink, and of him. He's only inches from me. Close enough to reach out and touch. Not that I'd ever dare.

I adore being near Rev. Touching Rev. Kissing him...

I swallow.

But those moments are painful because it's hope for the hopeless. It pains me every time I allow myself to fall into the wonderful oblivion of intimacy and then remember the truth. Even if Rev could somehow forgive me entirely, if he could somehow overlook the fact that I murdered his brother and destroyed his life, there's no way for us to be together. I'll never go home. I'll never see the sun without a haze over its lovely light. I'll never see the Shadow Court again. And soon, even Rev will be gone forever.

But the truth is, even if there was a way for both of us to escape this hell, there's still the fact that the rest of the realm will always villainize me. I could never be worthy of him.

My soul is scorched and rotting. My heart shattered and scarred.

Even if Rev could forgive me, I can't.

"I could stay here for a while longer," Rev says between long sips.

"We'd run out of food in a week."

His dark hair falls into his silver eyes, full of a sadness that kills me. His body is lean, his shoulders broad—but that's not what I'm supposed to be focusing on. I cast my eyes to the floor.

I was inches from death a few days ago. It doesn't seem at all right that I'd be basically back to normal this quickly. But when my ally has healing magic... well, that changes things. I shiver at the thought of his healing essence rushing through my body.

"We could forage for more." Rev shrugs. "That sorcerer stayed here for a year. It's obviously possible."

Theoretically, this is where I'll spend the rest of my days. That is, if I survive the quest we're about to continue. Even that seems farfetched, though, considering the fact that my death would stop the Night Terror's plan and save Rev... I'm not exactly holding my breath for a long life.

But if that thought makes Rev feel better—that I can have a life here after he's gone—I'll let him believe it.

I hop up and grab my backpack.

"You're eager to leave," Rev complains.

"Yes," I whisper. My magic is filled. My body healed. My heart is full, if not aching. I'm as ready as I'll ever be to continue this ridiculous quest through fae hell.

I'd happily spend the rest of my existence in this place with him, even with meager supplies and so few luxuries. But putting off the inevitable is not wise. It won't help us any.

I run my fingers through my hair and then tie it back in

a messy bun. I pull in a few long breaths, testing my newly healed body.

We can't just pretend the world isn't in peril and relying on us to save it. The scourge—a plague stealing magic and decaying our homelands—is still out there. Without the cure, the fae are doomed. It's become a lot more complicated with the new information we've obtained, but it remains true that the world requires the spell book hidden in the middle of these cursed lands. And we're miles from it.

"You know we have to go," I say, taking one last sip, savoring the calming herbs.

He doesn't respond. Rev still has a life waiting for him. A good life. An important role to fill. I won't let him throw it all away to stay in this terrible place forever.

That's my fate.

Not his.

"Cae," he says lightly, sitting on the edge of the bed. "I've been thinking..."

"Never a good sign," I say with a smirk.

He rolls his eyes. "Listen, you know I don't agree with my brother about... what he wanted."

My death. Apparently, I'm the key to setting the Night Terror free and reuniting with her powerful mate. If I die, their hope is lost.

"But, well, it's still true that the Night... whatever..."

"Terror," I whisper. "Night Terror." The other half of my own childhood nightmare. The Night Bringer trapped me and tortured me. I was only in his clutches for days, but that kind of pain and fear—well, that doesn't ever leave you.

Not one night has gone by without dreaming of his talons carving through my body. His deep rumbling voice, ancient and powerful, will haunt me forever.

And, yes, I'm planning to go face down with his other half—a being just like him.

"The Night Terror wants to trap you. Use you to undo her curse."

My eyebrows raise.

"She wants to capture you. Don't you think journeying toward her is a bad idea?"

"And she wants you dead. What difference does that make?"

"Maybe you should stay here. Let me go—"

"You're insane," I spit.

"Listen!" Rev says, holding his hands up in surrender. "Just hear me out. If you are still determined to come along, I won't stop you."

I roll my eyes because there isn't a thing he could say to keep me in this place while he risks his life to save the world.

"Reahgan had a point. You being out there is a risk. The closer you get to the Night Terror, the more likely she'll get what she wants. But if you stay here—"

"No," I say through gritted teeth. "No."

"You're so stubborn."

"And so are you!" I yell, tossing my hands up. "We're in an impossible situation. You think I don't know that? You think I don't realize that chances are I end up captured and tortured by—well, nearly, the same creature that captured and tortured me as an adolescent? You think that doesn't petrify me?" My breath shudders. I'm terrified of the day I enter his clutches again.

The Night Bringer can't touch me here. But his mate can. I'm not stupid enough to hope she'll be any better. She'll tear me apart limb and soul, the same way he did, then stitch me back together just enough to use me to complete whatever deeds they wish.

Rev steps forward, eyes softened. "Caelynn," he whispers.

I close my eyes at the intimate way he says my name now. I could die like this, just near him. With my name on his lips.

"I'm sorry..."

"Don't." I wave away his pity. "You have nothing to be sorry for. This is my reality. I don't dare feel sorry for myself, so you don't either, got it? I'll face my nightmare if that's what I must do."

I'll do it all over again just to save you, I think. I'd take the world on my shoulders, the hate and pain, and fear of a million years, just to know he is okay. Because my hope was lost long ago. There has to be a reason for all of it. If I let him die or fail or become trapped, then it was all for nothing.

Right now, what Rev needs is me alive. Me fighting. And so, that's what I'll give him. But when the time comes that I know that's not enough, things will change. I'll break his heart to save him.

4
REV

I stare wide-eyed and helpless at the beautiful shadow fae. Her face crumples, exposing her pain and fear for only a moment before she hides behind that shield of indifference once again.

The creature that captured and tortured me as an adolescent...

Her words ring through my mind, sparking a fiery rage in my chest. Beyond a rushed explanation during the trials —before I knew she was my mate— we haven't talked about what happened when she bargained with the Night Bringer. A bargain that resulted in her stabbing my brother in the heart.

That creature tortured her.

And I hated her for her choice.

I see her now, though, and I marvel at the depth within. She's broken and scared but also bright and hopeful. I only wish I'd seen it sooner.

The truth is, it's me I'm most angry with. Because I was so blinded by my hate that I never saw what she was. She was my savior. My fucking soulmate. And I'd condemned her without thinking twice. I'd tried to kill her, even while she was still working to save me.

Over and over and over again.

I thought she was evil, but now that I know the full truth, I can't help but feel like I'm the bad one. My soul is dull, cast in shadow, compared to the luminesce of her spirit.

Could I really allow some evil creature to take that away from me without fighting for it?

I can see the resignation in her eyes.

Caelynn still plans to die when the time comes. She'll drive the dagger through her own heart if she has to.

"What do you think will happen the moment they get to you?" Her jaw clenches. "If you're worried that, somehow, they'll capture me when we're together, then isn't it just as likely that she'll get her talons into you if you're alone?"

I let out a quick breath through my nose. "If I die, nothing changes. If they get their hands on you, they win."

"And you think I'll just sit here and let you die? You think I won't come running the moment I learn you're in danger? Those beings... they're smart. They know how we work. They know how we think. And I know myself well enough. I know that if they were to capture you." Her voice breaks. "I'd give myself up in an instant."

"To what end, Caelynn?" I ask, throwing my hands up. "You'll let the world burn to save my life?"

"Yes," she hisses, eyes as fierce as I've ever seen them.

I swallow. I... don't know what to think about that.

Would I do the same? Should I? Is it better to choose the realm I plan to lead over Caelynn?

"It will be all too easy for the Night Terror to capture you," Caelynn continues calmly, "and lure me in on her terms. You said it yourself: we're strongest together."

I bite the inside of my lip and nod. "Fine."

She lets out a quick breath. "Good." She doesn't so much as flinch as she spins to grab my bag. "You gave up quicker than I expected." She smirks as she holds out my backpack.

"I know a losing battle when I see one." I shrug and sling the bag over my shoulder. I still think it makes sense for Caelynn to stay behind. She's reasonably safe here in this magically secure cottage. And the farther we travel into the Schorchedlands, the more dangerous this becomes.

Unfortunately, we came on this mission remarkably less prepared than I'd thought. I didn't know how deep the conspiracy ran.

Was all of this—the scourge, the trials, the quest for a cure— all orchestrated just to get Caelynn here? That's what the wraith calling himself my brother had implied, but I have a hard time wrapping my mind around it all.

Or is this whole story made up? Maybe it's all a part of the Schorchedlands' attempt to derail us from our mission.

I don't know. That seems outlandish, but so does everything else.

As the story goes, the Night Bringer started the scourge and manipulated everyone into believing the spell book inside the Schorchedlands is the only cure. He pulled all the strings to get Caelynn into the trials. And he's been manipulating everyone to get her inside the Wicked Gates.

Because he needs her, and the book, to free his mate from this cursed place.

As for me? I'm only in the way. A tool he's used to manipulate Caelynn.

It's hard to say what I should believe. It's possible I don't even need the spell book to cure the lands from the plague. But I can't take that chance.

That's the only thing I'm certain of. One way or another, I'm getting my hands on that spell book.

From there, things get more complicated. Because I refused to leave without Caelynn. There has to be a way to get her out of here with her life still intact.

Or maybe... maybe I'll just stay. I'll deliver the book to the queen, say my goodbyes, and come right back into the waiting arms of the fae who gave up everything for me. We'll live a humble life in this little cottage, barely surviving, certainly not thriving, but alive and together.

It's cramped and old and dirty and nothing like what I've been accustomed to my whole life, and yet there would be a quiet kind of freedom. Choosing to live here.

It would strip my life of obligations and plans. I suppose I'd be proving my father right—giving him exactly what he wants. I can't be his heir if I'm trapped in hell.

What a sad ending that would be.

But if it's my only option, I may just choose it. Because I cannot live my life normally knowing I left her here. I can't. I won't.

Caelynn watches me, eyes narrowed, as I grab our last-minute supplies.

"What?" I ask.

"Nothing," she finally says and shakes her head. Then, she pulls the door open, making way for the sticky-warm air to blow through our pathetic safehouse. "Ready?"

I sigh. "No."

But even so, I step into the heinous terrain of the Schorchedlands.

5
CAELYNN

The ash-covered hills surround us. The black swamp, where we last saw Rheagan is behind us. Immediately, breathing becomes more difficult between the ash wafting in the wind and the rancid smell of rotting flesh and sulfur.

We pause, staring at the mountain pass before us. The Schorchedlands are not particularly large considering what's enclosed in these magical walls. It's all compressed into only a few dozen miles. It's built like a bullseye, with the worst terrain in the center. That's where we need to get to. The center of the map.

The distance from the Wicked Gates to the location of the spell book is only around ten miles, and we're halfway there. But bearing in mind the difficulty we've already faced—a bog of animated bones, a forest with white trees that show you your deepest desires and then trap you with their finger-like appendages, and a valley full of mindless wraiths and zombie bears—well, we're not exactly looking forward to the rest of the journey.

Rev glances over his shoulder, but I refuse to spend any time reminiscing or wondering. I keep my stare focused on the path ahead—literally. One step at a time if I have to.

We only make it five hundred feet before Rev stops. I halt beside him.

"Look," he says, his voice uncharacteristically somber. So, begrudgingly, I turn back.

The cottage stands right in the middle of a fairly flat valley a hundred feet from the swamp. The sky is streaked with reddish light and dark grey clouds where the silhouette of three wraiths descend slowly, cautiously, toward the rock valley and the cottage we left just minutes ago. This is the closest we've seen any wraiths come to the cottage, and they're steadily moving in.

While Rev's bright magic brings attention, mine is it's opposite.

Rev and I shift closer to the mountainside and I quietly wrap shadows over the two of us to keep us hidden. Using my shadows, I can become essentially invisible. Though it never works as thoroughly when I cast them on someone else. I can veil Rev, make it harder to see him, but that's the extent of it. It'll have to do for now.

"What are they doing?" Rev whispers. The wraiths converge on the cottage.

"They're making sure we can't go back," I whisper. The hair on my arms stands up straight. Which also means they've been watching us. It wasn't the magic of the cottage that kept the wraiths away. They were spying.

"They were watching us," Rev echoes my thoughts. "But not engaging. Why?"

I bite my lip and watch the wraiths gathering closer to

the house. They don't go in, but they shift around the structure as if examining it.

I press my lips together, mind whirling. "We should go," is all I say, and I spin on my heel to leave the cottage behind for good.

What does it mean? It means the Night Terror knew where we were the whole time. It means she's been keeping an eye on us and now doesn't want us to go backward.

It means she wants us to come to *her*.

———

We walk in silence for a full hour. I hold the thin shadow veil over us both, just in case. It uses up some of my magic, but it's not a full shield so the power required is minimal. As long as we're careful, we should be able to escape spying eyes.

"Can I see the map again?" I ask Rev. Unlike me, Rev had the chance to study these lands in as much detail as was available. Admittedly, the information is limited. There have been very few "expeditions" into this part of our world, and wraiths are not very forthcoming. They do seem to know a hell of a lot, though, which is incredibly annoying.

They know all our secrets but won't tell useful information until it pleases them. I wrinkle my nose as I think of my wraith... *friend.* I don't even know what to call him.

The son of the last Shadow Court High King and my great, great, great, great—whatever—grandfather, hasn't been around since I refused to abandon Rev to claim my heritage as the rightful queen of the Shadow Court.

"You've studied the map non-stop the last two days. There's nothing more to see."

I purse my lips, knowing he's right, but even so, staring at the spread of this terrible place makes it easier to swallow. Easier than facing the crumbling pile of rocks we're supposed to hike through.

There could be faster and less expected routes to reach the center, but from everything we've learned about this place, most of the terrain is next to impossible to survive—except for the one pathway built into it. The Bog of Bones was meant to be avoided—follow the rocks outside of the sewage-y swamp and the zombie bones won't bother you. The Forest of Desires had a clear pathway straight down the middle. The images inside the trees would tempt travelers to veer off so they could capture them with their clawing tree arms and suck their souls dry. I absently press my hand to my back. That wasn't a pleasant feeling. The wound still aches, more so than the wound in my stomach from wraith-Reahgan.

Have I mentioned my time in the Schorchedlands hasn't been very pleasant? Cause it hasn't.

Now, we have two and a half miles of mountains to traverse before we reach the wall of flames. The fae who built our cottage never traveled past the wall of fire. He didn't know how to get past it. Which, of course, bodes well for us now.

Only one known living being has passed all the way into the Schorchedlands, and he's basically a legend. No one knows the details. They just know he hid a spell book there. A spell book that can reverse the cursed plague spreading over the fae realm.

Without our wraith escorts, both of whom we've alienated by choosing not to kill each other—wraiths, apparently, aren't the most romantically inclined beings— we're flying dark. We'll have to work together to pass this new magical obstacle.

The hills are generally quiet this time of the day. Wraiths aren't fans of the light. Even though it's dull and hazy, they avoid the sun at all costs. I had been surprised at how little they've bothered us these last few days considering the Night Terror put a bounty on us. But now our recent wraith visitors tell me there is a very specific reason for that.

I just haven't figured out what that is yet.

Rev stops, holding out a hand to halt my movement. "Did you hear that?" he whispers.

Soft shuffling and scraping sound around the next bend. There is one large rocky hill standing between us and... something. Likely not wraiths since they float.

Were we in the fae realm or even on Earth, I'd guess it was a herd of animals. Deer or wolves most likely. But we are not in the land of the living any longer.

There are several different kinds of creatures in this place, wraiths being the most common. But there are also undead animals in various stages of decay. Some look almost like living creatures with greyed skin and open black wounds and the occasional exposed bone. Others are entirely skeletal with flesh just barely clinging to their bones in patches. But even so, the birds squawk, the bears roar and sprint and claw-like any other bear. I don't know how they're living or what made them this way.

Everything here wants to kill us. Including the passing birds that soar overhead.

"What should we do?" I ask. We know wraiths are likely following us, and if we face a group of zombified animals, we'll be forced to fight and will certainly bring attention to ourselves.

"We move forward cautiously."

"If we have to fight something... the wraiths will find us."

Rev nods slowly. "But there isn't another choice. We can't turn back now."

I bite my lip. He's right. I nod in concession but hold up one finger. "Let me handle it. My magic is less likely to catch unwanted attention."

Rev purses his lips but then nods in agreement. "Have fun," he says, waving his hand to usher me forward with a flick of his eyebrow. My stomach twists pleasantly as I meet his eye. Sick joy spreads through me at the thought of unleashing my awaiting magic. *Use me*, it seems to imply.

The memory washes through me—when I claimed my enemy's power as my own. When I murdered Rev's brother and completed the Night Bringer's "impossible" bargain. I won that game, a decade ago. And the Night Bringer's magic became mine.

I shiver at the pleasure that washes through me.

Killing feels good. That's a truth I learned a long time ago. A truth that haunts me daily.

I stretch my fingers, working to keep my mind in order.

My power can unleash—it can rage on our enemies—but it will never own me.

You are mine, I remind it.

It doesn't respond, though I hadn't expected it to. Once, that foreign magic could speak to me, instruct me. But the moment I succeeded in my bargain with the Night Bringer, it quieted and submitted to my rule. It hasn't spoken since that day.

I lick my lips and then march toward the unknown enemies around the bend.

6
REV

I pull in a breath as Caelynn marches forward. It was only days ago she was dying in my arms. Only days ago, she willingly allowed her life to end because she thought it would help us. Help me.

Now, my stomach squeezes tightly as she rushes out into danger.

Even without knowing what enemies lie before her, there is very little doubt that she can handle herself just fine. She's powerful. Determined. Capable.

To be perfectly honest, she's stronger than I am. Though, admittedly, I have an advantage here. My magic works exceptionally well against the dark powers of the wraiths, the downside being it's flashy and brings unwanted attention. But by simple raw strength, she has me beat.

So, I shouldn't be nervous watching her walk toward a fight on her own. But I can't help it. Dread constricts my lungs, suffocating me.

What if it's a trap by the Night Terror? What if Caelynn

purposefully allows herself to be harmed because she's still convinced her death is the best way to aid this quest?

Gravel and ash cover the uneven ground, with high, stone-covered mountains towering over the pathway. Shadows shift between the hills. My eyes dart around. I often notice a shift in the stone, but when I look there is nothing amiss.

I inch forward, a few feet behind Caelynn as she disappears around the bend to our unknown adversary.

A dull snarl rumbles. Caelynn's footsteps crunch over the gravel.

"Hello, beasty," she says before I sight the beast she's speaking to. A crunch, a crash, and a roar are followed by several more. Finally, the battle comes into full view and I see several wolves leaping at Caelynn, claws, and fangs first. Their rib bones are exposed, where slimy red patches of fur and flesh cling.

She spins, effortlessly avoiding the attack. Her blond hair falls free of it's binding behind her head and flings as she twists. Her iron knife slices through a white wolf's chest. It falls to the ground in a heap. She lands on one knee, her blade glinting with shimmering black blood.

Her eyebrow flicks, her expression smug and sexy as hell.

Three other wolves prowl forward, now wearier of their assailant.

"Run," she whispers. "Or die."

One wolf is a deep black with red glowing eyes. The other two are varying shades of brown, their eyes black as night.

These creatures are not wraiths. They are not even

necessarily evil—though I suspect these lands corrupt anything living here for very long.

The wolves bare their teeth, and Caelynn smirks, her eyes harsh and wicked. I stand back, now confident in her ability. In her willingness to win this fight. I can see it in her eyes. She's enjoying this.

My chest stirs with excitement watching her fight, watching her power and strength. Her slim body twisting with harsh yet elegant movements.

Black magic ripples behind her as she stands and three magic wolves of shifting shadows appear at her side. They match the three undead wolves, crouching and snarling.

"Go," she whispers, and her shadows made from swirling black power leap at the undead wolves. They clash for only a moment, a mesh of claws and teeth, and then the undead wolves yelp, turn on their heels and flee down the mountainside, the shadow wolves nipping at their heels.

I lick my lips, watching Caelynn watch them. The commotion of the fight fades away, and I approach the relaxed shadow fae. Her golden eyes dart to me, and she smiles.

She lets out a long breath. "That was fun."

My eyebrows are still higher than usual as I move to stand beside her. "I'm glad. It was... impressive." Although not at all unexpected.

"Never underestimate a shadow fae." She winks.

"Never again."

She smiles. We march farther down the path wordlessly, watching for the possible return of the wolves, but the mountainside remains silent and unmoving.

We stop at the edge of a precipice, looking out over the lonely road we've left to reach our next obstacle. Caelynn's blond hair rustles in the wind gently, her eyes cast out on the open lands.

This is her new homeland.

I remember when watching her reunion with the Shadow Lands. The pure bliss and utter pleasure that crossed her usually stoic expression.

Even the pleasure she shows now is a dull version of that moment.

My stomach sinks, and I swallow, looking away from her lack of emotion. She's at peace with her self-inflicted punishment. But I am not. I cannot stand the thought of leaving her here. How do I move on with my life, knowing she's here? Alone.

I shake my head and remind myself that I'm getting too far ahead of myself. First, we have to complete the impossible task. If one or both of us die, there will be no decision to make.

My chest tightens.

Focus on the task at hand, Rev. Your job is to get the book. After that...

I take in a long, deep breath. After that, I'll find a way to save her. I have to.

7
CAELYNN

After our short-lived battle with a few undead wolves, we wordlessly pick up the pace toward the main roads. Rev is the first to begin a jog. I casually press past him, and a simple smirk is all it takes to turn our journey into a race.

I don't dare use my shadow walking power this time, so it's just basic running. We pace each other, pushing each other. Yep, Prince Reveln of the Luminescent Court and I, practically frolic through the black mountains of fae hell.

What even is my life right now?

It's dark in the alleys below the looming mountains made of what looks to be solid black rock with a sprinkling of red stones. Some splotches are so covered in the red stones it appears like a splattering of blood. Part of me wonders if this was some wraiths art project once upon a time or if the terrain is just that morbid by nature.

The air becomes thicker the farther we run, the heat rising. The sky grows redder and redder until it's nearly glowing.

"Wow," I finally say through quick breaths as we slow to a walk. The smoke is thick here, making it even harder to see than usual.

There is a small precipice at the end of our current trail. Only around twenty feet below us is the flat ground of a smooth gravel path.

"You think that's the main trail through the mountain range?" I ask.

"I'm guessing that red glow up ahead is the flame wall. So yes, that's a fair guess."

"So, we should climb down, yes?"

Rev glances over his shoulder and then pauses. His eyebrows pull down.

"What?"

"I think one of the wolves may be following us."

I groan. Of course they are. "All the more reason to change paths, then."

I shrug. It doesn't make too much of a difference if those undead wolves decide to try for a little revenge. We can beat them easily. I'm more concerned with spies keeping an eye on us. If someone is following us, it very well may be a Night Terror lackey.

I don't like that we're moving exactly the way the Night Terror wants us to. I hate that she anticipates our every move. But I don't know what else to do. I don't know how to continue with the quest but not fall into her clutches.

Rev nods somberly, and I wonder if he's thinking the same thing. The climb down only takes a few seconds, and we're finally on the flat ground between two major mountains

We walk slowly now, knowing that if this is the main roadway, even the sunlight may not keep all wraiths from traveling here, and we are in open territory with walls of sloping stone on either side of us, where any manner of creatures could see us without us seeing them.

We keep close to the rocky edge of the mountain to our right, which limits our vision moving forward but also cuts potential sight of us.

Soon, it's hard to breathe through the thick blanket of smoke covering the mountain range.

Sweat drips down my back. Heat presses down on the both of us, and soon, the sounds of a flickering fire catch my attention. Through the smokescreen, the flickering red flames shift and pop. I stop, breaths heavy.

We knew the next obstacle was called the wall of flames, but I hadn't expected it to be quite so... literal.

The wall of flame stretches up into the sky at least a hundred feet high, and even beyond that, the plumes of black smoke rise farther than I could possibly see.

"What the hell?"

"Literally," I murmur.

He doesn't react to my cheesy joke, and I don't blame him. Now, I understand why the maker of our cottage never traveled past this particular obstacle... I'm fairly certain no living being could pass through a scorching wall of fire uninjured. Unless you're a fire fae, I suppose. Maybe they should have picked Brielle as champion just by default.

I've run through flame before and come out with only minor burns but that... well, this is different. That was a wall erected in a quick moment by an out of breath fae of average magical ability.

We are five hundred feet from the wall, and I'm already sweating. Heat radiates off of it. We won't be able to get within a dozen feet before it starts literally cooking us.

I stop, staring at the glowing red and orange flames.

"Think there is a way around?" Rev asks.

Shadows drift in and out of the flames, crackling and popping.

"This wasn't part of your research?" We'd talked about the wall of flame, but I hadn't thought to ask much about it, assuming it would be something like the Black Gates. To pass through, it uses its magic to mentally and emotionally torture the individual, and then they're good to go. But I'm not so sure about passing through this big guy.

"Not in detail. They certainly never mentioned a wall so thick no living being could pass through without becoming literal ash. That would certainly put a damper on this mission."

"Not to mention passing back through with a book in hand."

Rev narrows his eyes. "True. There has to be more to this."

A flash of shadow catches my attention in the corner of my eye. I spin to the place I swear I saw a prowling wolf, but there is nothing. The shadows beneath the mountain range remain perfectly still.

"What is it?" Rev asks.

"I thought I saw that wolf again. But I don't think those creatures could move that fast."

"Wraith?"

I bite my lip. "Maybe," I whisper. "We should find a place to hide for a bit. Catch our breaths and think this through."

Rev nods, and we slink to the other side of the pathway, away from where I'd seen the shadow shifting. Not far off, there's a narrow pass between two mountains. Single file, we walk into the narrow crevice of the black mountain. The heat dissipates gradually, aided by the shade cast by the cliffside. I can just barely see the smoke-covered sky from here.

We come to a sharp edge jutting out from the cliffside, creating a dark nook behind it. We're covered just enough we can settle in for a few minutes, confident we're not currently being watched. I drop my backpack and lean against the cool stone.

"So..." I drawl.

Rev chuckles. "I'd really like to get this stupid quest over with."

I pull in a breath. I know he meant to express his frustration with how difficult every step of this mission is, but my stomach sinks because I know the end of it for him doesn't mean the end for me.

I'm going to live the rest of my life here. I'll never see the clear sky. The bright sun. I'll never breathe fresh air or drink clean and cool water. I'll never see my homeland. I'll never redeem myself. I'll never get to thank the shadow sprites or tell the phantoms they were right about me and Rev.

"Cae..." Rev whispers. "I—"

I wave him off, knowing he must have noticed the tears welling in my eyes. "I'm fine. Just hits me sometimes." I shrug it off quickly with one shaky breath.

"Will you tell me?" he whispers then drops his bag at his feet and crosses his arms. "You're never open about what you're feeling. I just wish... I wish I understood more."

I swallow. "I was... just thinking about all the things I'll never see again." I shrug like it doesn't matter, even though we both know it does.

Rev's lips scrunch up as he considers his next words. "I don't know what the right thing is here, Cae. I don't know what the right thing to say is, but..."

"You don't have to say anything. I don't blame you. Not for one second."

"I know that." Rev steps forward, and his eyes flicker to my lips.

I blink back my surprise and my heart races.

"I don't want to say the right thing to make myself feel better, Cae. I want to give you hope. I want... I want you to know that I'm fighting for you now. Okay? You're not alone."

I pause, examining him. "What does that mean exactly?" My voice is hoarse as the breath leaves my lungs.

One side of his mouth turns up in a sad smile. "Cae, I do not intend to leave you here."

My mouth falls open. He... *doesn't intend to leave me here...*

That doesn't make any sense at all. "Of course you're going to leave me here."

He shakes his head. "You're not going to change my mind, so there's no point in trying. You're not the only one that can be stubborn as hell."

"But there isn't any way..."

A low, sinister chuckle echoes from the stone alleyway. I flinch and press closer to Rev, my thoughts flying from my mind and our conversation entirely forgotten.

I fling my shadows over us both, knowing Rev can't be entirely hidden by my magic. I can veil him, but the shadows will not dig deep enough into his essence. If someone is nearby and knows we're here, they'll see him. I'd been so distracted by Rev's declaration that I hadn't kept up our cover or kept watch for creatures following us.

"The humans have tricks, do they?" the voice calls with another cackle laugh. A form steps into view—white-grey smoke swirls and shimmers, holding the form of a prowling wolf.

My heart pounds, but I hold my breath. The wraith wolf's eyes dart around in the area he must have known we've been hiding, but he can't see us. Somehow, my shadows have done better than I'd thought they could under the circumstances.

I take a moment to examine our new adversary. He's nearly twice the size of the wolves I fought earlier today, but not as large as the bear we faced in the valley. I'm sure he's equally as formidable. He's speaking, which means he's more intelligent than the others. And the rippling smoke suggests he is not a simple animal—he's a wraith. He has magic.

The wraith-wolf prowls forward, his nose low to the

ground, sniffing, his tail wagging slowly. Well, it appears my shadows hide us from wraiths well enough.

"Worry not, children. I am not your enemy." His voice is smooth, unconcerned, but the look in his eyes tells me he's eager to find us. He's not a simply curious wraith.

He wants something.

His smoke billows up, making it appear like his fur is furrowing. Not exactly comforting.

Rev's hand settles on my lower back, pulling me in close.

"Still don't trust me?" he pouts, exposing a row of very real-looking sharp teeth. He chuckles again. "I just came down to help you through the wall, you see. It's quite easy."

I purse my lips, not even considering the possibility of trusting the wraith. For one—he's a wraith. I've done my fair share of trusting those creatures. Two, he came looking for us, and he's still searching, based on his movements. I grip Rev's forearm tighter, and we stand dead still.

Sweat drips down my nose.

"You don't want to know how?" the wraith says sweetly. His head lifts, ears perked curiously. "Very well, I'll let you walk right into the Night Terror's waiting claws by your own fruition—if you don't incinerate yourselves first, of course."

He turns, making his way back down the narrow walkway when Rev jerks forward. "Wait," he says quietly.

"Rev," I hiss through my teeth, pulling him back.

The wraith streaks in our direction, quick as lightening, his feet don't even move as he flies at us. I blast out acid, slamming into his snout. He yelps and skids to a stop, pressing his side to the cliffside opposite our hiding place. Teeth exposed; he licks at the minor wound on his nose.

The magical smoke making up his body dances causally, an eager expression on his inhuman face. "My humans have many tricks, I see!"

"We aren't humans," Rev mutters.

"Dammit, Rev, stop talking to him."

He knows where we are, but he still can't see us, and I don't intend to change that. The more Rev talks, the harder it is to remain hidden.

"You befriended a wraith just days ago," Rev complains. "And he helped you through several obstacles."

"That was different."

"We need to cross this insidious wall of flame, and he apparently knows how."

"Yeah, and he's also *very* interested in uncovering our hiding place. He wants something from us."

"Are you two finished with your bickering?" The wraith sits, chest puffed out. His shadowed head tilts back and forth like he's more doll than sentient being.

"No," I say. "But you may as well fulfill your apparent worth before I kill you."

"Not very friendly humans." He tsks.

"We aren't humans," Rev says again. "We are fae."

"Same thing, child. Living beings are all stupid and controlled by their whims." He spins slowly in a circle, pacing in front of our shadowed hiding place.

"How do you get through the wall," I say impatiently.

"Ahh, yes, the obstacle looks simple enough. The heat

and crackle suggest it will simply sear the flesh from your bones, but appearances can be deceiving."

I roll my eyes. "So, it's worse than searing flesh? That's good news."

"Not worse. Not better. Only more complicated."

"How?" I say again. "How do you pass it?"

"You walk."

"And it won't kill us?"

"Oh, it may. But it will not harm your body."

I blink.

"This is spiritual fire, not literal. It will not burn your flesh. Instead, it scorches your soul."

"Well, that sounds pleasant."

"Oh, it is not. But, torture or not, there is a purpose to the pain. Fire is not meant as punishment, not solely. No, fire is a purifier, you see," he says. "You pass through the fire, and it will measure your soul. It will show you how to live without the weight you carry. How to heal your wounds and clean your blemishes. You will survive if, after the pain and fear and anger—the darkness of your spirit— your soul is intact enough to appease the flames."

My eyebrows pull down. "So, it... burns the bad out of your soul?"

"No, no. Not so simple. That would imply you will no longer have that weight once you pass. No, you must go through the process of healing yourself. It simply measures you. Judges you. It shows you your faults. And pushes you in the right direction. If you are not worthy, you will disintegrate into your own guilt. If you are worthy, you will continue no different than before—at least physically."

"Worthy," I repeat. "That doesn't even make sense."

"Of course it does."

"No," I say back stubbornly. "That's where the Night Terror is, isn't it? How did she pass through the fire? You're telling me she has good in her?"

"Oh, no. Not at all. That creature is as evil as they come."

I lift my hand, palm up.

"Haven't you wondered why she hasn't yet come to find you herself?"

I tilt my head.

"She's sent wraiths after the living but has not joined the hunt personally. That is because she cannot pass through the flames. She is trapped in the innermost circles."

My mouth falls open. I suppose that does add up. "So, is she trapped by the Wicked Gates or by the wall of flames?"

The wraith shrugs. "Both. Though, I suspect she could dismantle the flames if she was so inclined. Her motivation has been lacking over the years of her banishment. She has only recently begun moving again. Slithering inside the darkest places of this dark place."

I bite my lip as I consider this new information. I wouldn't have chosen to trust this wraith, but we're here now. May as well make the most of it.

Finally, I drop the shadow veil. The wolf grins.

If his information is correct, then I wasn't all that wrong in my guess that it's not unlike the Black Gates, which makes one live through the feelings and thoughts of their death. Will this make me relive all of my regrets? All of the darkness in my soul? What if that drives me insane? What if there is nothing left when I pass through?

That will be worse than death. If my soul is disintegrated, I won't even have the chance to become a wraith. I'll be gone forever. I'll cease to exist.

Regardless, I must try or let Rev face the Night Terror alone. Not an option.

The bad news is that this also means the moment we pass the wall we'll be within reach of the Night Terror. I didn't admit it to Rev, but I am terrified of the moment I face her. Will she be like the Night Bringer? Worse? A creature trapped in this torturous place for hundreds of years... I'm sure she's not exactly pleasant.

I knew we were walking closer and closer to that reality. But something about knowing we are safe from her direct reach now but not once we pass the wall makes it feel more real. Will she be there waiting for us the moment we pass? Will there be an army of wraiths waiting?

"See for yourself if you do not believe me. Creatures will pass through the fire as they would pass through a smokescreen. There is no trick. There is nothing you can do to ensure you survive. You will either pass or you will fail. You will not know until you're beneath the roaring flames."

"Or you could just be telling us this to ensure we both die." I place my hand on my hip.

The wraith tsks. "I have given you the knowledge I have of the judgment. You must choose your way for yourself."

"We tried to get close already, and my clothes began smoking."

"Such exaggerations." The wolf rolls his eyes. "The

real trick for you will be passing through without falling into a trap. The Night Terror and her beast are waiting for you."

I bite my lip. "I figured that much."

"Well, I could possibly be persuaded to help." The wolf begins to pace again.

"What would you get out of the deal?" Rev asks.

His smile spreads wide, exposing those sharp teeth again. "The satisfaction of knowing I helped to end the Night Terror's reign."

I narrow my eyes. "You told us you weren't an enemy," I say. "You didn't say you were an ally."

"Oh, well, I'm not, strictly speaking. I simply haven't chosen a side. If I believe you capable of succeeding, I would love to align with you."

And if he decides we are doomed to fail? What will he do then?

I glance to Rev, who's watching my expression closely. "What do you think?"

We got as much information out of the wraith-wolf as possible, so we could run or fight or just tell him to shove off now. Or we could accept him as an ally. Because I do agree we could use help to ensure we aren't falling right into the Night Terror's clutches the moment we pass through the wall of fire.

"I think our next step is scoping out the wall," Rev says. "He says wraiths and animals pass through the fire as simple as a smokescreen. Let's see it."

I purse my lips. A test. Or at least stalling. I suppose I can handle that decision. I nod, and for the first time, I drop my shadows.

"We're going to journey closer to the wall," I tell him. "To watch something pass through."

"Well, what are you waiting for?" he exclaims. "Let's get a move on."

The wraith-wolf prowls forward, leading the way back through the mountain pass. I am not particularly confident in this wolf's motives being so pure, but I will admit we needed information. If there is one thing wraiths seem to be good at—it's information. How they seem to know everything, even about specifics outside the Schorched-lands, I'll never understand.

"What even are you?" I ask as we walk slowly toward the wall of flames. Heat is already building. Sweat beads on my brow.

"Me? I am a wraith, of course. I thought you were smarter than that."

I roll my eyes. "Why do you take the form of a wolf instead of a fae? Are you something like the zombie animals we keep seeing?"

"Those mindless creatures? No, certainly not. They are simply animals unlucky enough to have been trapped in this forest when the curse began. They were living breathing beasts once upon a time."

I frown. They were regular animals when the Schorchedlands were created? I can't imagine them being able to breed, so did they become immortal when they were trapped? I blink back those thoughts. I have more important things to consider right now.

"I take the form of a wolf simply because this was the form I died in."

My eyebrows pull down. "What?"

"I was a shifter, child. From the Beastly Court. I took the form of a wolf as often as I pleased. It was a convenient form to take for battle. And that is how I died."

"Interesting," Rev mumbles.

Finally, the roaring red wall of flames comes into view and I am reminded of just how uncomfortable it is to be near. "Why is it so hot if it doesn't burn you physically?"

"It is meant to be intimidating, child. For living beings especially. It was not made for you. Though you can, of course, pass through it."

"Of course." I roll my eyes.

"You can believe me or not. That is a choice you must make. I am surprised though," he drawls. "Why are your wraith allies not helping you in this challenge? Did you get them killed with your stupidity?" The wraith's smoke swirls over his eyes in a strangely haughty way.

"They are both alive," I say with no intention of expanding. There's no telling if this wraith is a spy only seeking to gain information.

"They are not friends," Rev says. "Both have abandoned us."

"I wouldn't be so certain about that. Kin have a way of sticking around, for better or for worse."

"Reahgan was kin, the other was just a strange tag along," Rev says.

"Ahh, so your mate has not yet told you?"

My eyebrows pull low in a grimace. "How do all of the wraiths seem to know so much?"

"Told me what?" Rev asks, his expression hard. "What didn't you tell me?"

"Nothing important," I say.

The wraith chuckles. "No, nothing important at all," he drones, clearly sarcastic.

"It isn't. It changes nothing." The fool wanted me to use his information to betray Rev, but that will not happen. I am here. I am trapped. I will not have the opportunity to put his information to any use.

"Caelynn..."

I toss my hands up. "Wraiths. Always have to make everything so difficult. The wraith was some great, great, great relative of mine, and he wants me to claim the Shadow Court's heritage and make it strong again. Obviously, that's not happening. So, again, it *doesn't matter.*"

Rev is still examining me, his eyes narrowed, but he doesn't speak. Yes, I'm withholding some information. I'm not yet ready to admit that I'm technically the true heir to the Shadow Court throne.

I'm not taking that throne. So, it doesn't matter. I don't even want to think about it.

"Who was he—the wraith?" Rev asks, his eyes darting to the wall and back to me. "Does he have something to do with the reason the Night Terror wants you?"

The ground rumbles beneath our feet. More of the magic of the flames?

I nod and cross my arms. "I didn't even get his name, but he was the fae who placed the curse on the walls surrounding this place so that the Night Terror would remain trapped. They need someone of his blood to reverse the curse. Someone powerful."

Rev searches my expression, but I won't let him see the emotion beneath the surface. It was all their fault. My court was systematically weakened over the last several generations all because of the Night Bringer.

Another shudder runs through the mountains, stronger this time. Like thunder. It's a quick boom, then it fades away.

"What is that?" I whisper, eyes shifting toward the flames.

"A powerful creature," the wolf-wraith whispers, so low I almost don't hear him. My heart hammers in my chest. His eyes are wide as he stares at the wall.

One more boom sounds, and we begin stepping farther away from the fiery wall, down the main road, wondering where we should move.

"So, that's why they've targeted you. But it's been centuries. Why now?"

I bite my lip. "The shadow fae have had their magic purposefully bred out so we wouldn't be strong enough to reverse the curse."

Rev's eyes narrow. "Until you."

"Perhaps we should take this conversation elsewhere," the wraith says suddenly, for the first time sounding anxious.

I nod both to Rev and the wraith. I don't know what's making the thunder-like sound, but I don't mind *not* finding out. We begin a brisk walk away from the magical wall, back down the main trail.

The wraith looks back then forward, his shoulder's tight.

"Until the Night Bringer gave me some of his magic, yes." That was what changed everything. I was as weak as anyone else in the Shadow Court. I couldn't have broken the curse either. Until I made a bargain with the Night Bringer. I was tortured into agreeing of course, but part of the deal was taking some of his magic. That magic helped me to kill Reahgan, a fae much stronger than me otherwise. The Night Bringer didn't expect me to succeed in the bargain—he wanted me to fail. I'd have his magic, but he'd have control of it and therefore of me. I'd be his slave. And I wouldn't have had any choice but to obey his every word.

Then, I would have had the power needed and I'd be under his control. Win-win for the evil being.

But because I did succeed and killed the right fae, I have his magic and I'm free from his torture and influence. Now, they have to find a new way to use me.

The wraith wolf freezes mid-step. "Wait... what did you say?"

I turn to face him, noting his slacked expression. Honestly, it's sad that I'm becoming accustomed to reading the smoke bodies of the wraiths. They have no real physical form, it's entirely magic pretending to be physical. But I suppose I should get used to it. I'm going to be here for a very long time.

"What?" I have no energy left to play games with him.

Something I've said has fear coursing through him now. His chest pulses with it. "You have the Night Bringer's magic?"

"I thought you wraiths knew everything?" I roll my eyes. "Yes, he gave it to me in exchange for a bargain. But he only did it because he needed me to be strong enough to break the curse."

The wraith slowly backs away. "If the Night Bringer's

magic is inside of you... then, you've already lost. It will control you. Strangle you from the inside."

I shake my head. "I've had his magic for over a decade. It once had a mind of its own, sure enough, but since I completed the bargain, it hasn't so much as whispered to me."

The wraith's eyes narrow. "He wouldn't have given it to you if he didn't intend to use it against you."

"I am certain he intended to use it against me, yes. But that doesn't mean he succeeded."

The wolf crouches, baring his teeth. "You think you've won? That his plans aren't much larger than all of this? No. No, I hadn't chosen an allegiance before now. But I will not pick the losing side."

The flames flash black then back to golden-red. The wolf's eyes grow wider.

"Wraith!" a voice echoes over the flames. The very ground rumbles beneath my feet. The mountains tremble, and my soul along with them. "It is your time to *choose*."

The final word echoes over and over, bouncing off the stones towering over us.

The wolf crouches, baring his sharp fangs. The terror in his eye matches mine.

"No," I whisper. Because I know that voice. It's different than *his*, and yet, the same. The stone recognizes these creature's dominion. The world quakes with their voice.

I know I should run, but my muscles are frozen. My mind is clenched with fear—memories echo through me.

Night Bringer.

Master.

It was so long ago that I'd faced him. So long ago that his talons carved through my body and spirit. But I can feel it. The echo of wounds long since faded.

I barely even register as claws and fangs fly straight at me. Instinct takes over, and I fling shadows at the wolf, but panic constricts my breath, and my magic flickers weakly. The wolf easily dodges my attack and reaches for me. His claw slashes through my forearm, and a cry of pain escapes my lips.

Then, a wall of light stretches between us. The wolf roars in pain and rage as he slams into the glistening whiteness. I, too, shrink back at the bright light, eyes searing.

Rev roars as he swings his arms, and his magic mimics the motion, sending the wolf flying toward the cliffs. The wolf's smokey magic slams into the stone, and he falls limp to the ground.

The ground rumbles beneath us, louder and stronger. Faster.

"He's coming." The wolf whimpers.

I find myself on my hands and knees, unsure how I even got there. My fingers dig into the soft clay-like muck. I can't breathe, can't think. All I can hear is his voice.

The Night Bringer.

The rumble of eerie distant laughter pulses through me, and I can't tell if it's real or memory.

I dig deeper, fingers curling into the soft ground. I close my eyes, frustrated with myself for my reaction.

It's just a voice.

But then—half a mile away—the fire shifts, exposing a creature three times the size of an elephant. Its skin is thick and scaled, with a mane of thick black fir around its head and shining horns darker than the blackest night curl over its ears. Its eyes glow red. *What the hell is that?*

Strong but gentle hands grip my waist and yank me to my feet. I stumble, trying to follow his guidance, but my shaking legs rebel, knees buckling. Rev tugs me into his arms as he sprints away from the beast and the wild flames.

Rev races down the trail, carrying me. We curl around the side of the mountain, rushing down the first path we pass. I cling to Rev's shoulders and focus on his sharp breaths. His heart hammers into my side.

Several minutes later, Rev slows to a walk. That creature—whatever the hell it was—didn't follow us. I'm fairly certain we could hear it coming for miles.

"Can you walk?" Rev asks as we find a smaller pathway. I nod, and he gently sets me on my feet, his arm still curled over my back. I hold onto his shoulders for a moment longer, our chests touching.

I swallow.

My cheeks burn red. I'd had a panic attack right there as a wraith was attacking me. *Good timing, Cae.*

I swallow. Maybe that was the point. Maybe they knew the moment I heard her voice, I wouldn't be able to cope. I'd fall apart like a little china doll. Pathetic.

Rev's hands rest on my waist, nose grazing my hair. He waits for me to pull away.

I breathe deeply, taking in his comforting scent of sage and cedar. How he still smells good after nearly a week in this place is beyond me.

Then, I pull back and force my body forward down the trail. Rev follows my lead.

My steps are wobbly for a few moments, but I pull in all my determination and find a solid rhythm. I focus on each step, one at a time. I don't know where we're going, and to be honest, I don't much care so long as it's not back toward the flames. Gaze cast to my boots skidding over the ashy stone walkway, I chant over and over that I'm okay. We're okay. Both of us.

And this time, if I have to face the Night Terror, I know I won't be alone.

8
REV

Caelynn stumbles her way through the winding trail, deeper into the mountain range. I have zero intention of going back toward the flame wall today, not even to try spying like we'd planned. And I don't suspect going back to the cottage is wise either, even though it's only another mile or so from here.

"I thought he was helping us," I say quietly, resisting the urge to pull Caelynn back into my arms.

"He might have been. He changed his mind," she says, and I shake my head in disbelief. Caelynn was right about trusting another wraith. We did get useful information, but it almost cost us our lives.

Now, we've got to figure out if anything out of his mouth was accurate and what that will mean. He did mention that the Night Terror was waiting for us to cross the wall, which would mean even if he's right—that it's a simple stroll through a magical field that weighs your soul and then let's go—we have to be very careful when and how we venture across.

We have to be ready for a fight the moment our feet land on the other side.

I place my hand on Caelynn's back, gently guiding her through an opening between two smaller mountains. The stone here is uneven, the path meandering up and down and around haphazardly. There's evidence of recent landslides, shifted stones, piles of rubble, and an arrowhead-shaped trench carved into the mountainside.

Which probably means this pass is treacherous and we should avoid it, but that's the exact reason I lead us in this direction. Falling stones are the least of our worries in this part of the world.

If we pass through this uninhabitable area, we may be able to find a safe place where the wraith spies won't expect us.

It may or may not work, but it's worth a shot.

We walk another half-mile north, where the stone grows larger and more settled. The sky is back to its patchy grey with a red tinge. Much preferred to the scarlet glowing red it becomes by the wall of flames. There are no paths here, which is all the better. It means for a more challenging walk, but Caelynn's feet grow steadier and steadier as we go.

Finally, I find a small nook between rocks.

"Do you think this will keep us safe for the night?" I ask.

Caelynn looks up for the first time, her eyebrows pull down then up. Then, she nods. "It'll do."

She steps forward, fingers sliding against the damp stone, and she crouches inside the small opening. Then, she presses her back against the barrier and slides down.

She slumps over her knees, face pressed to the crook of her arms.

"Are you all right?" I whisper, watching her from the cave mouth. I want to comfort her. I want to take care of her. But I have no idea how to do any of that.

She nods without looking up.

The cave—if one can even call it that—is tiny. It's covered on all sides except one small opening, but it's only about four feet deep and two wide.

My cheeks flush as I consider what that will be like for both of us to try to lie here.

In the cottage, we'd shared a bed, but it was large enough we didn't have to touch if we didn't choose it. And most of the time, we didn't choose it. Well, she didn't choose it.

"We have a long time before sunset," I mutter. We left early in the morning, and we've spent a few hours traveling, but that leaves many more hours in the day.

She nods, finally pulling her face from its hiding place. There are bags beneath her eyes as if it's been days since she last rested.

"I'm not sure I'm in a proper state to cross that fire wall, though." Her voice is hoarse.

I wave her off. "Of course not—that's not what I—"

"Even if it's as simple as the wolf made it sound and we cross easily due to the goodness of our souls or whatever..." She winces, fear flashing in her expression. Is she uncertain about the state of her own soul? Does she not see what I see? "We're not sure what's on the other side of it, and the Night Terror..."

"Was that her? The voice?" I ask softly. The ground-shaking, bodiless voice. It was unnerving, for sure, but it didn't affect me the way it did Caelynn. Or even the wolf for that matter.

"It sounded just like *him*," she whispers.

I'd heard the Night Bringer's voice once before. At least, I think it was him in the Cave of Mysteries during the trials, but I can't say for certain it wasn't just a trick. But either way, the fear of my memories doesn't cut as deep as hers do. "That's why you..."

"Freaked out? Yeah." She swallows and looks down at her hands. "I suppose it brought back a few memories."

My chest tightens. *The creature that captured and tortured me as an adolescent.*

"You've never really told me about it," I mutter, lowering into a crouch. The ground is damp and tough, with uneven stone.

Caelynn never tells me anything I don't need to know. She hides what she feels, what she thinks, what she's done, and what's happened to her. I want to know her more. This... well, it's easier to not know. But I want to. I want to know what she's been through. I want to understand what I once thought was inconceivable. Unforgivable.

"Will you tell me?" I whisper. I don't ask if she wants to tell me because I know she doesn't. "What happened to you?" I ask for the first time.

Caelynn bites her lip, eyebrows bent low as she considers. She shrugs, and I press my hand to my heart, feeling it pound uncontrollably. I'm eager and terrified.

"How did you end up in a bargain with him?" I prompt because she hasn't outright turned me down, and I know this is hard for her.

"One night," she begins slowly, her voice low, "I overheard my parents talking about sending me away to another court." She clears her throat, and her voice becomes steadier. More confident. I can practically see the emotion fading as she straightens her shoulders and tucks it all away behind those shields she's so proficient at wielding. "I didn't understand that conversation very much back then. They talked about me not being strong enough. I just thought they were punishing me. But now I think they knew. They knew that the Night Bringer was following our bloodline, waiting for the right person to come along that he could use as a tool to break the curse. Because I had the right blood, I was in danger. Actually... I *was* the danger." She shakes her head.

I don't speak. Don't move. I long to comfort her, to take away all of her pain. But I'm far too late.

"They knew," she whispers, eyes unfocused. "I remember their expressions after the queen banished m,e after they learned what I did. I remember them saying *banishment is better*. I never knew what that meant, but I guess now I do."

I swallow. "Banishment meant being away from the Night Bringer's reach."

"Mostly," she whispers. "But yeah, I guess it's because they knew he'd gotten to me."

I swallow.

"I thought they hated me. They wanted to disown me. Well, maybe that's still true. But maybe it's not. Maybe... it was what was best for me. Get me out of the realm and out of his reach."

I take in a long breath through my nose and let it out slowly.

"So, anyway... I ran off to complete my first rite of passage without their permission. If I just completed one, then they couldn't force me to move away or marry someone at another court. But it was there that the Night Bringer found me. He tricked me into one of those small tunnels. And..."

I swallow.

"He made it very clear what my life would be like if I declined to take his bargain."

I pause, every muscle tense. I can barely breathe. "He tortured you."

She pauses, her face slack, emotionless. Then, she shrugs. "I took the bargain. And he sent me to a ball to meet you. He knew what you were to me. I'm certain of that."

Silence stretches between us, just the rain pattering gently outside. When did it start raining?

"You ever think about what things might have been like?" I ask, watching her closely, memorizing every feature. Who would she have been, if... "If the Night Bringer didn't even exist."

Her lips lift into a gentle smile. "I spent ten years thinking about that."

My face falls, and I press my eyes closed as shame washes over me.

"What?" she croaks.

"I spent ten years imaging your death," I say. "You spent ten years imaging our life together."

She purses her lips. No hint at all she has any idea why this is significant.

"It's a wonder you're the one we call a monster."

"Rev," she says firmly. "I *was* a monster. I killed a fae prince. Good or bad, it doesn't matter who he was. I killed him. And he was your brother. I would never even dream of blaming you for hating me." She shakes her head. "*I* hated me."

The breath that escapes my lips is shaky because I can relate. I've hated me too. My life was so full of anger. At myself. My father. The girl who took my brother from me.

I strove to prove I was worthy of my title. Worthy of my brother's legacy. But unlike Caelynn, I had a scapegoat. I projected all of that on her. The fae that wielded the blade that ended my brother's life.

If only I'd know it was all to save my life.

"Were you ever going to tell me?" I mumble.

Caelynn blinks. "What?"

"That he hurt you." I shake my head, my thoughts are jumbled and confused. Images flashing through my mind, of Caelynn during the trials. She knew. The whole time, what I was to her. And that I hated her. I wanted her dead.

Why didn't she ever tell me?

Her lips part. "The Night Bringer? Why would I—"

"No, I mean my brother."

9
CAELYNN

I suck in a breath. "What?" I breathe.

"Were you ever going to tell me that my brother hurt you before you killed him?" His words are forceful, like an accusation. I flinch.

"No," I say firmly.

He presses his palm to his lips, eyes soft and so achingly sad. I don't want Rev to ever be sad. I want him to be happy. That's my last wish. The last thing I'll ever be granted.

I will find a way to win this fight and save Rev so that he can go on and live a good life without me. My own life was forfeit a long time ago. All I've ever been able to ask for is little moments of happiness. Of friendship and giving hope to someone else. Seeing it in their eyes. Hope for life that I never had.

Or, well, haven't had since I was seventeen. That feels like a different life altogether.

I shake my head from those thoughts and wipe the tears. When I look up, I see Rev watching me. Our eyes meet and they stay that way, locked but neither of us speaking for a full minute.

It's an eternity, this minute. Bitter but sweet. And I'd take it. If this were all I could have. If moments like this were all I could steal away from what could have been between me and Rev... I'd take it.

"I wish you'd told me," he says finally breaking the silence.

"Why?" I whisper. "It would have only caused you more pain."

He takes in a long breath, pulling his eyes from mine. "You let me believe you were a murderer. Even up to just days ago. I thought... I mean I guess I kinda knew. But I still let myself believe it. That Reahgan was good and you..." He shakes his head.

He wouldn't have believed it, if I had told him. But I don't say that.

"Why would I want to hurt you more?" What good would it do to tell him that his brother used his power to hold me down and told me how he'd torture me. That the guards and the High Court wouldn't care what my body looked like when he finally gave me up to the authorities?

I shiver at the thought. No, I wouldn't ever tell Rev that. Not even now.

He thinks it somehow justified what I did. And while it certainly made it easier—I'm not convinced I wouldn't have done it anyway.

Another reason I'm not so sure I'll make it through that wall of flames that apparently destroys you if it deems you unworthy.

We're quiet for a long time, just listening to the pattering of the rain outside.

"It drives me a little crazy, thinking how I'd judged you. How I hated you for so long. I imagined your death more times than I care to admit. And it's funny now, I have those same dreams sometimes. Where I kill you. My hands are wrapped around your throat and I squeeze the life out of you, or I carve out your heart the way you did his."

I ignore the clenching pain digging into my chest and force my face to remain neutral. *He still has those dreams.*

"Only now," Rev continues in a near whisper, "those dreams are nightmares. I wake in a cold sweat, panicked that you're gone. Guilt-ridden that I'd done it."

My lips parted in surprise. Gone is my mask of indifference, though I couldn't possibly name the emotions running through me now and so I have no idea what my expression tells him. I watch as he speaks to the ground. Puddling with pools of water.

"If only I'd known," he whispers.

"Rev..."

"I'm sorry," he tells me, dark eyes flashing to me.

"What?"

"I'm sorry for thinking those things of you. I'm sorry for hating you."

"Stop, Rev."

"No," he says, eyes watery. "I hate that you went through all of that. I hate that you spent your whole life protecting me while I only made it worse for you."

"Stop!" I shout. "I am not some saint, Rev. I deserved my punishment. And you did nothing wrong."

He shakes his head. "I thought you were evil. I let

myself believe it because it was easy to hate you. But I saw what he did to you, or part of it, during the first orb challenge. I didn't believe it. I refused to see what was right in front of me—"

I bite my lip. "Rev, you were wrong to think me evil, that's true. But you're wrong now too."

He pauses. "What do you mean?"

I sigh. "I'm not evil. But I'm not good either."

His eyes pierce me, the way he always does, and I look away.

"My soul is tarnished. Scarred. Deformed. He was right. The Night Bringer, when he trapped me... he told me things about myself. He said I was like him. That I desired power. That I thirsted for it. That I'd bring pain to the world to achieve it. Those things scared me as much as he did—because he was right."

Rev's eyebrows pull down.

"I am a victim. In a lot of ways. But I was selfish and stupid and power-hungry and vengeful too."

Rev stares down at his hands as he wrings his fingers.

"And you think I'm not?" he says, his voice husky and pained all at once. "You think I didn't choose power over... shit, everything else. You think if I had a monster whispering in my ear that if I complete one terrible deed, I'd have all the power I'd craved—that I wouldn't have done it?"

I swallow. "Would you?" My voice breaks.

"I don't know. It would depend on how it was presented to me. But I don't think it would have been difficult to make me cave."

I lean my head back against the stone. A drop of water

lands between my eyes and I flinch. The cool water is a welcome distraction though.

"You didn't know me before the trials, but you saw some of it. You saw how power-thirsty I was. How I'd plow through anyone to achieve my goals. How I'd destroy anything in my path to prove myself."

"And how many people did you kill?" I ask sharply. I don't need him to convince me that what I did wasn't bad. I don't even want that. I just want this conversation to end.

"No one. But I didn't save any either. You did."

"Rev," I bark.

He waves his hands casually, willing to give it up. "All I'm saying is that—" he pauses and purses his lips like he's choosing his words carefully. "You and I are mates for a reason. Fate doesn't make that big of a mistake."

My eyebrows pull down in confusion. "What?"

"Maybe we both belong here," he says finally.

10

CAELYNN

Rev sits beside me, quiet and still for—I don't even know how long. Long enough for the gentle rain to stop.

Rev and I are so complicated it's hard to keep these lines straight. We are allies. And friends. We should be lovers, but that will never happen. So, we pretend. Pretend that this is all there is.

I pretend that I'm not watching his fingers curl over his thigh, measuring the space between us. That I don't think about his lips on mine about every ten seconds. That I don't wish there was some way that I could be good enough for him.

The awkward silence stretches between us. He knows I'm hiding from those deep conversations that lay me bare. Things I don't ever want him to know. Burdens that shouldn't be his.

I force myself to my feet suddenly, crawling from the tiny cave in an instant. I just need to move, to get out of this tiny, cramped place, but my knees buckle, and I lose my balance. Rev must have followed me out because his hands are at my waist, steadying me.

My cheeks burn in embarrassment. Why? Why do I have to be so weak now? Like poison in the air is seeping into my lungs. The magic inside my veins crawls like little needles piercing everything.

"Careful," he whispers, his tone husky, and just like that, my mind is spinning through what I want him to do. What I wish we were, could be.

My back presses against the nearest stone, and he follows, ensuring I'm okay.

I don't know if I am.

His silver eyes are stark against the dim and sour red of the Schorchedlands' sky. His hands are on either side of my head.

"Caelynn," he whispers. His voice sends every rational thought fleeing from my mind. His eyes flicker from dark to silver and back, like he's unsure what to feel. I swallow, unable to take my eyes off of him.

My hands move—of their own fruition, I swear, because I never consciously decided to touch him this way. My fingers slide up his stomach, feeling the ripples and curves of his muscles, up over her chest to his shoulders.

There, that's a safe place to stay.

He steps closer so that his hips rest against mine.

"Rev." I groan. My eyelids flutter closed as his warmth seeps into my skin, making me realize how cold I'd been. How starving I'd been.

Starving for him. Starving for his touch, for his closeness.

I grit my teeth, knowing that's not true. Knowing it

can't be true. I can't need him because I won't have him. Rev is not a possibility.

But then, his fingertips glide up my arm and my head falls back against the stone. His thumb hooks inside the strap of my tank, gliding down, and a gasp escapes my lips. He pauses, fingers lingering at my neck. I resist the urge to look at him—to find out why he'd dare stop—because part of me is relieved.

He lets out a breath and then gently grips my chin. "Look at me."

I oblige. He's so close, his nose inches from mine.

"I know..." He winces, a myriad of emotions flashing over his features. "I know everything sucks right now. I know this world has never been kind to you. I know you've let go of your hope. But..." He licks his lips, and my stomach flips irrationally. "I want to give some of that back to you if I can. I want..." He closes his eyes. "I don't know what the right thing is. But I do know what I want..."

My chest heaves, hardly able to get enough air through my aching lungs.

"Will you tell me what you want? Not forever. Not in a week or a year. Because I know that's impossible to know right now. I know you refuse to hope for more than right now. So, tell me, now, what do you want?"

I swallow, my heart throbbing in my chest. Tension in my gut rushes down, making my head spin. I want him. I do. But I'm so beyond terrified of wanting anything that I don't think I can have...

He examines my expression closely, seriously. His eyebrows pull down, and pain flickers over his expression. Then, slowly, he pulls away.

My first instinct is to pull him back, to wrap my arms and legs around him and hold him in a damn vice grip, but my fear closes over my throat, and I don't move. I don't stop him as he crouches to reenter our cave, taking his warmth with him.

And I don't say a damn thing as he hides his pained expression from me.

11
REV

I endure another long stretch of awkward silence and consider the wisdom of taking another trek out to the wall. We need to gather more information, but that creature—

I shiver.

And Caelynn seems so weak after that fight.

We can't sit here forever, though, and I find myself restless. The sting of rejection still lingers. She doesn't want me.

Or maybe she does, but she's too stubborn to admit it.

The wolf-wraith is still out there. I could have killed him. Should have, I realize, but I was more preoccupied with making sure Cae was okay than anything else. And by the time I got her to her feet, the wraith was gone. Vanished from the place he'd fallen.

I didn't want to freak Caelynn out any more than she already was, so I didn't mention that fact and just quickly moved us to as safe a place as we could get. We are only a few miles from the cabin, which is now being watched by wraiths. Maybe it's even been destroyed by now, for all we know.

To waste time and occupy my mind—anything to stop thinking about that rejection—I pull out the map of the Schorchedlands and stare at it absently.

"Think of something new?" Caelynn asks.

"No. Just bored." I drop the thin paper to my lap. Caelynn needs to recharge, and it seems best for us to wait out whatever the other that creature was. Tomorrow, I fully intend to scope out the flame wall, see if we can find some evidence that the wolf-wraith was telling the truth. And if so, we'll then make a plan on how we can cross with at least an attempt at gaining the element of surprise.

Until then, we wait. In the tiny, cramped cave.

"Well, let's talk through what we know we have to do," she says. "First, we cross the fire wall. Risk of death or not, we pass through the damn thing."

My eyebrows rise.

"After that, there is a swamp, possibly a forest, and one single mountain right in the center of it all. It's only a three-mile journey from flames to spell book."

"Simple," I say and smirk. "Should be easy."

"What do you think the swamp will be? Flesh-eating bacteria? Dismembered limbs? Blood sacrifice?"

"A swamp filled with thick warm blood," I say because that sounds exactly like something this place would hold.

Caelynn shivers, and I chuckle. "That's disgusting. You're probably right."

"The farther we travel, the worse it's supposed to get. And I don't suspect they mean by gross factor."

Caelynn nods. "It's hard to imagine it getting worse than what we've already faced."

I agree but don't bother to say the words. This place has lived up to my every expectation. Including the fact that my mate is trapped here with me and only one of us can leave.

Can't get much more tortuous than that.

Aside from the whole man-eating trees and corpses brought to life, I shudder to think what else might be waiting for us beyond that wall of flame. Other the obvious —Caelynn's personal nightmare monster.

I wring my hands, wondering if there is some way to convince her to stay. She shouldn't have to face this. This time, it's my turn.

"Caelynn," I say, low and slow.

Her eyes linger on my lips for a moment then move up to mine. "No."

My heart sinks.

"I'm not staying behind."

I shake my head. "It doesn't make sense for you to keep going, Cae. For so many reasons. You don't need to do this. It's not your fight, not this time."

Her head falls back against the damp stone as she stares up at the narrow rock above. "It's both of our fights."

"You've done enough. You've faced them already. I want to save you from this."

"I'm sorry, Rev. But you can't. Neither of us ever had a choice, but this was thrust on us. I can handle it, okay? I can and will face the Night Terror when the time comes. I'm scared, but I'm not afraid."

My lips curl into a sad smile. "What's the difference?"

She shrugs. "My mind knows I'm scared of them. Panic still hits sometimes. But my heart is willing because it's worth it."

Her determination to save me is strong enough to overcome her fear. Or maybe she's just too damn stubborn. Why does she care so deeply for my wellbeing but continues to push me away physically?

"But what if you didn't have to?" I ask. "What if I'm capable of doing this on my own?" Caelynn is brave and strong but stubborn as hell.

She narrows her eyes, watching me. "Maybe you could. But I don't think you understand what being left behind would do to me. On the other side of the wall was one thing—when I didn't know what monsters you were facing. But to expect me to sit here and do nothing. To just wait, even while knowing she's coming for you—a creature more powerful than both of us even understand—trying to kill you." Her bottom lip trembles, and it's like a knife to the gut. "I can't."

"Okay," I whisper. I hate it. I don't want her putting herself at risk when it's something I'm convinced I could do alone... But I can understand why it would be incredibly difficult for her, so I concede. Because if it were me, I'd fight too.

12
REV

Caelynn slips into a restless sleep less than an hour later. I watch as she curls up awkwardly on the damp soot. I gently pull her hair from her face and tuck it behind her ear, if only so it doesn't fall to the mud-caked ground.

I consider, not for the first time, if maybe Caelynn isn't as healed as I'd thought. She was on the brink of death only days ago. Wraith magic carved a hole through her chest and grazed her heart. Maybe that had a larger effect on her than I'd thought possible.

Physically, she should be fine. My magic is fully capable of stitching up every inch of her. It can search her body for anything amiss.

Her chest rises and falls, her muscles flinch periodically.

So maybe... maybe what's happening with her isn't physical. Maybe it's mental. Maybe it's magical. I don't know. Maybe she doesn't want to live anymore.

My stomach clenches at that thought. This female has

me wound like a top. Physically, I want her, but she won't reciprocate. Which would be fine, except I'm convinced she wants me just as badly. Emotionally, I'm compelled to protect her and care for her. I cannot fight this urge to save her.

And to be honest, I'm long past done fighting it.

I'd once thought it was only the magic of the mating bond—something mystical that was entirely out of my control. But I know better now.

That was just an excuse.

Now, I know she's perfect for me. I press my eyes closed as a new wave of pain washes over me. She's the one. My perfect partner. I'd kill for her. I'd die for her.

I don't deserve her.

But I don't know how to do this right. She pushes me away. She draws me in. She deserves so much more, but she's not willing to fight for it.

I turn to the gentle glow of light shining from the opening of our tiny cave. I'm glad Caelynn is getting the rest she clearly still needs, but I'm restless. Eager for answers. Dying to *do* something.

Now that Cae is resting, maybe it's a good time to do a little bit of spying. Without her shadow magic, I'll be more exposed, and I'll have to travel at least two miles south to reach any place I could get a vantage of the wall.

I'll risk running into that crazy looking creature. Is it guarding the wall? Will it remain there so long as we are seeking a way to cross?

My knees ache from the awkward position I've stayed in for the last hour, and if I choose not to go exploring now, I'll be stuck in this little hole for another twelve hours.

Once the sun goes down, we won't have a choice but to hide away.

I'll go crazy if I don't stretch at least a little bit.

The rocky hillside has been dead quiet since the moment we arrived here. There's always the possibility that something is watching us, but that remains true no matter if I stay still or take a walk.

I crawl out of the cave and take a moment to stretch and then examine the hills around us. The sky above is hazy red, like constant fog. I realize now that the red is likely due to the wall of flames considering how bright the entire sky got as we'd drawn closer to the magical force field.

The two mountains towering over us are tiny in comparison to the rest in this range. The main trail that leads from the valley to the wall of flames is half a mile west. There's at least one large mountain between.

The stone is lighter here, more grey than black.

It's too far to go all the way to the wall without Caelynn, I decide. I don't want too much distance between us. But I begin to walk in that direction slowly, sticking close to the stones just in case I'm being watched.

The gravel crunches beneath my feet as I get closer to the nearest trail, where part of the path is blocked by fallen rocks. There are tracks along the sides of the mountains here, where landslides have occurred. Rivulets of rainwater trickle down the slope, slipping into cracks and fissures.

I stop when the gravel pathway comes into view. I shouldn't go any further.

I'm itching to move forward with my quest, but moving into the open isn't a wise choice, not without

Caelynn at least. I stop, though, when a few speckled flowers catch my attention. Around fifteen feet up, growing out of the side of the darks stone is a set of four scarlet flowers.

I smile. Also, probably not worth the risk. And yet, I'm going to do it anyway.

I make the climb in three fluid leaps, careful to keep my next landing place planned just in case any of them give way. I grip the flowers between my fingers and rip them violently.

I'm back on the flat valley ground, flowers in hand, in only a few seconds.

"Lovely, but oh so foolish." The deep voice sends shivers down my spine.

I spin to face a wraith blocking my path back to Caelynn.

13
CAELYNN

My head throbs, pounding in waves. I groan. My cheek sticks to damp dirt as I pull myself up. *Well, that's not a very pleasant way to sleep.*

I blink, heavy lids barely able to open. The uneven, curved opening to the cave appears as a gentle glow. Everything else is pitch black.

It's daytime. It wasn't night when I fell asleep, so that may mean it's only been minutes. Maybe a couple hours. Or maybe it's been an entire day. Who the hell knows?

The next thing I realize is that I'm alone. I jerk upright, causing a wave of nausea to wash over me. Where is Rev? I scramble out of the cave, muscles roaring in protest.

"Rev?" I croak through cracked lips. "Rev!" I say louder, risking exposing our hiding place, but I don't care.

I look up and down the valley we fled to. Ciffsides rise a few hundred feet into the sky, jagged grey stones jutting out here and there, and on the gentle slope of the valley floor, there are a few patches of grey grass. No paths, no sign of life. I don't even remember getting here. I press my eyes closed. Rev isn't here. Not at all.

He left me.

Panic rises in my throat.

He asked me to stay behind, and I explained how I couldn't do that. How it would kill me. But he went anyway. He went to try to save me from the Night Terror. Or maybe it was to take the glory for himself. To say he did it by himself.

I shake my head. It doesn't matter what his motives are. It doesn't matter what he feels about me, about the world outside these scarred lands. What matters is that he left, and I am going to find him.

My mind settles enough for me to think things through a tad longer, and I realize my forearm is aching. Throbbing. Burning.

I rip up my sleeve and find an open wound where the wolf clawed me. In my very non-physical panic, I'd forgotten about the injury. I don't even think it bled, but... my flesh hangs open, blotches of red skin sagging and grey. That's not a trick of the light, right? It's not a natural color.

I quickly pull the sleeve back down and push the sick feeling away, a sour taste in my mouth. Rev brought me here then left me behind. Determination swirls in my gut. I'm going to figure this out.

The sky is a scattering of shades of grey with a red tinge. To my right, the sky glows the brightest. Bright red. The flame wall. That's where he would have headed. I don't let myself dwell on the what-ifs. If Rev tries and fails to cross the wall. If he's found by wraiths or worse, that horned creature. I shiver.

No, I focus on the anger. I focus on what I must do.

I sprint in the direction of the red glow.

I will find him, and then I'll kick his ass for daring to leave me behind.

———

"Tell me why I shouldn't kill you now, foolish child." The voice trembles in simmering rage.

I follow voices that mutter angrily just around the corner...

"Do you think she'll just turn back and do as you wish because my heart has stopped?" Rev asks. "If so, you do not know her very well."

"Oh, but you do? The mate that rejected her?"

Deep black smoke forming the shape of a man in a wafting cloak comes into view. Anger fuels my magic, swirling in my palm. Ancestor or not, I am ready to destroy him for threatening my mate.

"Move away now, wraith," I roar, lip curling.

The wraith spins as I pull my arm back to attack. He hisses and twists away from us both, stopping feet away.

"What are you doing here?" I ask, seething.

"Helping," he says, his eyes narrowed, watching my hand still poised to shoot him with my shadow magic.

"You've made it very clear that you are not our ally. So, sorry if I'm hesitant to believe you."

"I am your ally, Caelynn of the Shadow Court. I am simply not his." He points to Rev.

"Which makes you my enemy. Now, leave before I kill you."

"He was just taunting me, Cae." Rev steps forward, hands up in surrender. "He didn't—"

"I don't care what he did or didn't do." I bare my teeth at Rev, feeling wild. Hot rage thunders through my veins. *Destroy.* "And don't you dare think I'm not also pissed at you."

"Me?"

"You left," I spit. "After everything we talked about, you were leaving without me."

Rev's mouth falls wide, his eyes soft but large. He's surprised. "No, Cae, I wasn't. I just got restless and went for a walk. I was going to come right back."

I turn my attention back to the wraith.

"Trouble in paradise?" He grins.

A sound rips from my chest, and I throw my shadow ball straight at him. He hollers as it slams into his chest, and he flies back into the stone fifteen feet back.

My chest heaves, rage still simmering, but I allow him to pick himself back up.

He exposes his teeth. "Are you done yet?"

"Are you?"

His eyes are narrowed as he slithers closer, drifting right and then left. "You are changing," he whispers.

"Caelynn..." Rev's soft voice drifts through me.

I put my hands down. I allow my muscles to relax, and I face him.

"Are you okay?"

I cross my arms, my rage drifts away. I am tired. I am sad. I am still a little mad, but... I shrug.

Rev approaches me like a spooked animal, and I resist the urge to roll my eyes.

"I'm fine," I say. "Just mad at you."

He reaches out to rest his hand on my shoulder. "I'm sorry. I promise I wasn't leaving you behind. I wouldn't do it. Not like that."

I purse my lips. "Well, then, you were just being an idiot."

He huffs a bitter laugh and smiles. I loosen a deep breath, expelling the rest of my tension.

"What about him?" I nod to the wraith.

"I'm not sure what he's here for. I don't think he was planning to harm me."

I wrinkle my nose. "Good. I still don't trust him."

"Did you come to help us cross the fire wall?" Rev asks hopefully. "We could use an ally." His hand slides down my back.

"Of course not."

My lip curls. "Then what? What purpose could you possibly have?"

"I will not help you cross the flame wall because you will certainly perish the moment you do."

I roll my eyes. "Then what, pray tell, do you suggest?"

"What do I suggest?" the wraith drifts closer, his smokey magic billowing. "I suggest you turn back. Caelynn goes through the gates to the land of the living."

"And leave Rev behind."

"It is the only way." His eyes remained narrowed, as if unsure if I'm safe to approach. I haven't ruled out the possibility of attacking him again.

"You're a coward. And you think me one if you'd bother to even suggest such a thing."

"It would be a very brave thing to do, child."

"No. No, it wouldn't. Because it wouldn't solve anything. The Night Bringer would still try everything in his power to control me. He'd still find a way to torture me. He'd find a way to win. I'd lose Rev just to keep fighting this same battle elsewhere."

"You do not see how very close to defeat you already are, child." His voice is soft now, concerned.

"If I die, then they lose. Rev can still complete the mission and save—"

"No," Rev growls in my ear. "That is not a solution."

"There is no solution!" I throw my hands up.

The wraith narrows his eyes again, drifting closer, and then circling us. "Days ago, you hated her, Prince Reveln."

"I was angry and hurt. I didn't ever want anything bad to happen to her."

Rev pulls me in closer, and I let him because his warmth sends shivers through my body.

The wraith's eyes turn eager, pinned to Rev. "Perhaps we could come to an agreement…"

"No," I snarl, done with this conversion. I don't need him manipulating Rev into doing what he wants. No. It's not going to happen. "We've made our decision. If you don't intend to help us complete the mission, then you are not on our side. You are not our ally or our friend. So, leave. I don't want to hear what you have to say."

The wraith stops, chest puffed out. "Very well. I can see you are a lost cause."

I cross my arms and watch as he drifts away, up, up, up, and over the mountain, along with scattering ash and dust, until his form disappears completely.

14
REV

The wraith disappears over the mountainside, but my eyes are pinned to Caelynn. We left the cottage less than eight hours ago, but already her eyes are sallow, her face pale, and her posture defeated.

"You mean it?" she whispers, still staring up at the mountain. "You weren't going to leave?"

I grip her upper arms tightly and spin her to face me. "Of course not." My jaw tenses. "I promise. I won't leave you if you promise not to leave me."

Her lips part. Confusion flickers across her expression, then finally, the tension drains from her body and she nods. But there is no joy in her now. It's resignation, as if I'm asking something terrible of her. As if continuing to face the pain of this place is a torture she'll endure for my sake only.

She steps away from my grip. "How long did I sleep?" she asks as she begins north toward our current camp.

"About an hour." I fall into step beside her. "We still have four or so before sunset, I'd guess."

"Let's grab our things and head toward the wall. We can find a place to see without being seen."

I frown. "You're up for that?"

She nods.

I'm not sure what the right choice is. Clearly, Caelynn needs... something. Rest. A break. Hope. But I'm not sure what sitting in that stone nook will achieve toward that goal, and getting information on the fire wall is important.

I let the silence settle between us, only the crunch of rubble beneath our boots sounds around us for the next few minutes. We reach the cave, and Caelynn ducks in first. She assembles our abandoned supplies with renewed purpose, and I just watch her for a few moments—there isn't room for both of us moving around in that little nook anyway.

She shoves my blanket inside my backpack hastily. Followed by a sheathed dagger—I have two others strapped to my body—and a water bottle. She zips it up and tosses it to me.

She finishes grabbing the rest of the supplies and crawls out of the hole. She slings her own pack over her back. "Ready?" she says, already stomping south, but I grab her arm to stop her.

She frowns. "What?"

I step closer, towering over her, finger gently gripping the lapel of her leather jacket. "Are you really okay?" I whisper.

"Yeah," she says, her voice high pitched. A lie? I narrow my eyes. She looks more energized than before, livelier than even minutes ago. Maybe she is okay. But I can't shake the feeling that something is wrong.

"You're sure? Nothing is… wrong?"

"Everything is wrong." She lets out a bitter laugh, but her shoulders slump, and one side of her mouth tips into a small smile.

"I mean, besides… everything." I rub the back of my neck. Everything is wrong, she's certainly right about that. I knew my time in the Schorchedlands would be torturous, but once she showed up, things grew significantly worse. Now, my only chance at completing my mission will mean leaving my soulmate behind in this terrible place. Not my *only* chance, I remind myself. I'll find a way.

"I'm fine."

"Nothing hurts? There's nothing I can do to help you?"

She purses her lips, and then her gaze flickers down to her forearm.

"Let me see," I demand.

She scrunches up her nose. "It's nothing. Just a scrape from the wolf attack."

"Let me see," I demand again.

She sighs and then drops her backpack and rips her jacket off her body, leaving only a cotton shirt, stained with brown and red. She pulls the sleeve up carefully as it sticks to greyed flesh.

My stomach roils as she exposes a gaping wound on her forearm. "Cae…" I gasp.

She frowns. "It wasn't that bad before," she mutters. "I don't think."

"Sit," I bark. "In the cave, actually." I shake my head. We've got to be smart about this. She needs to be healed before we head out into dangerous territory again.

"You don't need to heal it," she says half-heartedly.

"Have you seen it?" I exclaim. "I can see your bone, Cae." Not only is the wound large, skin and flesh torn away, but it doesn't look right. It isn't red and swollen like I'd expect. It's colorless, white flesh and darker in certain splotches, appearing grey. Like her arm is... dying. In only a few hours since the injury occurred.

"It looks worse than it is. Doesn't even hurt."

"We are not going back out there until I heal it."

She grumbles and scoots back inside the cave. I drop my backpack and pull my own jacket off, then I drop to my knees.

She gasps, eyes wide as I crawl toward her. My eyes flit over her body. Shit, not supposed to be thinking about that sort of thing right now, Rev. *Caelynn has a potentially fatal wound. Make it better. Then you can think about fucking her.*

I swallow and refocus. Caelynn resettles, sitting cross-legged, and offers me her arm. She concentrates on something over my shoulder. A gentle shield of shadows washes over the entrance to our cave. Blocking anyone outside from being able to see my glow of magic.

I grip her wrist gently, and my left-hand warms immediately without even needing to concentrate. My magic is ready and willing to heal my mate. My eyelashes flutter as the light rushes into her open wound, searching and clenching, stitching the tears in her flesh. It takes very little concentration to enter her this time. Now, I know her. I feel her. Caelynn's dark energy washes over me. Her magic mingling with mine. I feel her pain, her bravery, her thirst, and fear. Her hope—a gentle glow so gloriously beautiful it takes my breath away. But that light is flickering, barely hanging on in a storm of raging winds. It's cold. So cold.

My magic rushes forward, seeking to devour the cold, to warm her, to—

Caelynn rips her arm from mine, and I blink back to reality. Unbearable heat returns, my skin prickling with sticky sweat. Her eyes are wild, pained. She holds her arm to her chest tightly, leaning away from me. "What was that?"

My lips part. "I don't know," I whisper.

She blinks rapidly then shakes her head. "Let's go."

"Your arm is okay?"

She turns her arm over, skin pink and healthy.

"Okay. Let's go." We gather our bags, but I pause. "Will you promise to tell me if you're not okay?"

Her eyebrows pull down. "I don't know if I can tell anymore."

15

CAELYNN

Rev is quiet, standing just a foot behind me, watching the roadway that leads to the fire wall.

We'd spent a full hour wandering the mountain west of the wall to no avail. We reverted back to the smaller mountain tucked between the larger two and finally found another small cave near a cliff where we can see the pathway leading to the flames.

We'll have to walk a dozen feet around the corner to reach our sleeping place, but that might be a good thing. So, we've settled down on a large sturdy rock to stare at the flames for a very uneventful hour.

The area is still. No sign of wraiths. No shifting shadows or distant sounds. Nothing.

Then, breath catches in Rev's throat, and I shift my gaze just as the fire ripples. A tiny opening unfolds and out hops a rabbit.

I blink and grab Rev's hand to notify him of what I've seen without making a sound.

An undead rabbit, rib bones entirely exposed with one

floppy ear, bone and sinew hanging off of it, hops a few steps beyond the flames causally. As if the fire holds no danger whatsoever.

It stops to sniff the air then freezes.

Its pitch-black eyes shift to the ledge we're on, and my breath catches. A moment of quiet stretches as all three of us wait. Then, the rabbit darts toward the rocks and disappears into some unseen crevasse in the mountainside.

"Did it see us?" Rev asks.

"Yes," I whisper, watching the place it fled. "Maybe we're not as inconspicuous as we'd previously thought."

"You're using your shadow magic?"

"Yes, but only a veil, not a full shield. It would take more energy for that."

He pursues his lips. "Should we use more shadow magic?"

I bite my lip. "Probably. But that comes with some drawbacks. It'll drain my power pretty quickly if I cast a full shield day in and out."

"We can rely on my magic for offense. Yours for defense." Rev's light magic is impressively effective against wraiths, so it does make some sense. But I hate the idea of weakening myself and having to rely on him to defend me if an attack comes. Not that I can't fight without magic, even entirely drained, I'm stronger than most of the creatures we come across. So long as there aren't too many of them. I picture the clawing skeletons from the bog piling on top of Rev.

I remember that helpless feeling because I couldn't reach him in time. Well, I could have. Would have if I had to. Back then, I had an ally helping me. Sort of. He would have happily watched Rev drown in that smelly muck. Just like in my dream, he wants me to leave Rev behind.

That wraith that called himself my ancestor is pretty high on my list of enemies. I put him just behind the Night Terror because she's the bigger threat. I'm not sure where I should rank the Night Bringer because he's not here inside these walls and he can't get in. Even so, I'll never forget him. The way he hunts and waits for the right moment. Luring fae into his trap.

I shiver.

"So, what now?" I ask. We can only wait here for so long.

"We still don't know how to pass through the flames," Rev answers.

"That rabbit crossed without so much as blinking. Maybe it's not as formidable as we think."

"Look at where we are," Rev says with a flat voice. "It's more likely to be worse than we think, not better."

"So, what? We just keep putting it off? We try to figure out some puzzle we only have one piece to? We have to make the leap, Rev. We can't just wait this out. It'll only get worse."

Rev winces. "We can gather more information by continuing to watch."

"How? What do you think we could find out?"

"Maybe we should have talked with your wraith ancestor. He could have—"

"He could have purposefully gotten you killed. That's what he's most likely to do. He isn't trying to help us, Rev. He wants something from us, just like everyone else." I swallow and look past him toward the glowing wall of red fire, eagerly lapping into the sky like fingers reaching for something to burn.

"I'll go," I say.

"What do you mean?"

"I'll go first. If I don't disintegrate into ash, you can follow." Easy solution if you ask me. It's certainly possible I'll die a very painful death, but at the end of the day, that's better for the both of us anyway. Well, I mean, I'd prefer a painless death, but that's never been a likely option for me anyway.

Rev clenches his teeth, his jaw muscle popping. He steps forward. I cross my arms, holding my ground, but my heart races. It always does when he gets this close.

"What do you think your chances of survival are?" his intense grey eyes pinned to mine. I feel like that rabbit facing a predator. My magic is stronger than Rev's, but he has power over me that I cannot control.

"Slim," I admit, forcing my stare to remain solid.

His fingers grip my chin. "Why do you wish for death, Caelynn?"

I close my eyes, suppressing a shudder. "You said you want more information. You know we need to cross the fire. We can't wait forever. This is doing exactly what you're asking for in a way that limits the risk. That's it."

"Limits the risk," he mutters, shaking his head. His jaw ticks. "If we're taking huge risks with our lives, why not talk to a wraith?"

I step back, lean against the rocky hill behind us, and slide down to my butt. "The risk of talking to a wraith is that I get captured and taken to the Night Terror. I'd rather gamble with my death."

"Then, I'll talk to them. They don't want to kidnap me."

"No, they want to kill you."

"That's the same thing you're willing to risk. Your life or my life. My plan has more likelihood of success if you ask me."

I pinch the bridge of my nose. "You're impossible."

"Tell me, how is it different?"

I frown but meet his intense stare. He knows how it's different, he's just digging for a response.

I lean my head back against the stone and stare up at the hazy sky. "Because you need to live."

"And you?"

I grind my teeth. "I know what you're trying to pull out of me, and yeah, I think it's better for everyone if I die. Okay? Reahgan was right. If I'm dead, they can't use me and their plot ends. They lose, Rev!" I'm shouting now, and I don't even know how that began, but my emotions are exploding. The pain and regret and rage and fear, all of it pours out of me. "There's no winning against them. But we can make sure *they* don't win."

16
REV

I brush my knuckles against Caelynn's cheek, wiping away tears streaming down. I've never seen her cry, I realize. She's seen me cry. She's held me while I melted down.

"There has to be a way," I whisper. There has to be.

She presses her eyes tighter. She doesn't want to live any longer, and for some reason, that scares the hell out of me. But it's the pain and rage that simmers inside of me that's most surprising. "I never took you for a quitter, Caelynn of the Shadow Court."

"I'm not quitting..."

"Sure you are. You're giving up on yourself. On me." *On us.* My stomach churns.

"No." Caelynn shakes her head. "Never on you. This is for you. All of it."

"Well, stop it," I say firmly. "If you die, I'll never complete this task." I say it as motivation for her, but as the words leave my lips, I realize I believe them. This is too big for me. I could survive the Schorchedlands on their own. But against an army of wraiths? Against an ancient creature imprisoned here for centuries because the leaders of that time couldn't control it?

Truth be told, it's probably too much for both of us. But we have to try.

"Maybe it won't matter," she says, sniffling. "Maybe once I'm dead, the Night Terror won't pursue you or the book. What would she have to gain at that point?"

"Yeah, you're right," I drawl. "Those creatures don't at all seem the kind to desire vengeance or to kill for the hell of it."

She lets out a bitter chuckle.

"Maybe there's another way to cure the lands like my wraith said," she shrugs. "Like the gates implied. Maybe you could leave now, forget the wall of flames, go back to the fae world without the spell book, and..."

"And take the gamble that if I don't have the power to cure the lands—a concept that seems pretty damn far-fetched as it is—that no one could get the spell book out of here for another decade? I won't do that. You know I wouldn't."

Caelynn takes in a long breath but doesn't give me any more arguments.

"If you die, I'll die trying to complete the mission. Because then, maybe someone else can come after me and complete it." I plop down on my butt and sit beside her. "Don't leave me, Caelynn," I whisper, voice huskier than I'd intended.

She whimpers. "Okay," she finally whispers in return

———

Caelynn and I sit still, watching the quiet road below us for another hour without speaking. No other creatures come by the wall of flame. No wraiths, no bears, no wolves. There aren't even birds who fly over the barrier.

"Let's stay here for the night," Caelynn says, breaking the silence.

I don't respond. We have enough time to retreat to our previous cave. It's smaller but safer. Here, we are so close to the main road, so close to the fire. Its hot, dry heat presses in on us. Sweat clings to my clothes, making them stick. Just a mile north, we'd be significantly more comfortable.

"We haven't seen much of anything because this is when the wraiths all sleep. If we find a place to hide, I'll use my shadows to keep us hidden throughout the night, and maybe we'll get the information we need."

"You can do that? Keep up your magic to hide us throughout the whole night? Even hiding in that cave, this close to the wall, we aren't entirely safe."

She nods. "I'll only need to cover the opening to the cave, which will conserve energy. We'll be able to see out, but no one will see in."

"It'll mean staying up the entire night, won't it? You're not capable of controlling that magic while you sleep, I assume? I don't want to underestimate a shadow fae again, but that seems—"

Caelynn chuckles. "It will mean staying up all night,

yes. But we want to keep an eye on the road anyway. I already napped today. I'll take another once the sun rises, and then we'll decide what our next step is."

Our next step. Caelynn still intends to experiment with the fire wall with her own life. We do need to cross the fire, but there is no way I'll let her go alone. We'll go together or not at all.

17
CAELYNN

My soul aches, raw and open. Sore, like my arm isn't the only thing that was injured in today's adventures. And well, maybe it's true. Darkness, toxic and scary, clings to the edges of my consciousness.

Shadows are my element. My friends. But here... here, it's so much different.

Maybe it's just because I've mentally and emotionally chosen to die—I'm just waiting for the right moment. Or maybe it's something else.

Rev sits still and quiet, staring out the opening of the cave, into the shadows beyond. The sky is growing dimmer every moment, but this place is so dark to begin with it's hard to tell when it's officially night, at least visually. When we begin to hear the moaning of the dead, that's when I personally declare it to be officially night.

My muscles throb. My head pounds. Maybe staying this close to the wall was a bad idea. I probably could use more rest, which is rather annoying considering I shouldn't need more rest. I slept plenty in the cottage. More than my share, if I'm honest.

Something about these lands drains me of energy. And though I won't tell Rev this, the thought of using my magic basically every moment in order to hide the two of us sounds excruciatingly exhausting. But I'm going to do it.

I'm going to do it because we need it. Because I need it.

So far, the darkness has been sneaking over the mountain pass, inch by inch, but we have yet to see any more movement on the pathway below. The undead rabbit aside, we've seen nothing of note. Over an hour has passed since either of us last uttered a word.

Rev watches the scene before us, still and stoic. Stubborn or loyal. There isn't much of a difference. He's so determined to protect me, keep me from harm even though it's far too late. I've doomed myself. That ship has passed. But I suppose I can appreciate how difficult it would be to watch someone you're growing to care about die, hopeless to help.

He can't save me. No matter how hard he tries.

I'm just going to have to go along with his hopes until I'm certain his quest can be achieved. Until he no longer needs my help. Then, I'll find a way to slip away quietly and allow him to go on with his life.

This is just another thing I know Rev needs from me. To believe there is hope. To believe I will continue to fight.

"Caelynn," Rev calls quietly. "Come look."

I inch over to the ledge opposite the cave and peer over his shoulder. Down the rocky cliffside, shadows shift eerily. "Wraiths?"

Rev shrugs. "How's that shield?"

I take in a long, deep breath. My magic is solidly around us, but it takes constant effort to sink it deep enough to cover Rev and I both so completely.

My breath shakes as I take in another. My shadows have always been my protectors. But lately, it's felt more like a burden.

We revert to the cave, where we can only barely see the pathway below. We can't see the fire wall beyond.

My stomach aches as I force the magic to dig deep. I've never been able to shield someone else the way that I can with Rev. I can use shadows to cover something, but there is a difference between shielding something and merging shadow with flesh and bone. True invisibility only comes with oneness with the shadows. Only a shadow fae could achieve this, or so I thought. Because yesterday with the wolf wraith, he couldn't see us at all.

Either wraiths have worse eyesight than living beings, or despite how we both continue to fight the bond, my magic recognizes Rev as my mate, and his magic recognizes me. Theoretically, the closer we get, the easier it will be to use our magic as one.

Rev shivers as the magic settles over the cave, but then he pauses, studying me. Can he tell something is off? Can he see how exhausted I am?

His silvery grey eyes hold mine for several moments. His lips part and I expect him to speak, but nothing comes out. Instead, his fingers inch toward mine. The first moment his skin contacts mine is like a spark. I let out a breath because even that tiny connection reminds me of what I'm here for. What I'm fighting for.

I haven't given up on him. I won't. Not ever.

18
REV

Caelynn's eyes are so faded and lifeless. Her magic settles over me, but it feels... weak.

"Do you think there's something to what the wolf said?" I ask, surprised by my own question. It's something I've been considering for the last few hours.

She frowns. "What do you mean?"

"He said the Night Bringer gave you his magic and he'll use it to... I don't know what he meant but... to control you? Do you think... being here...?"

Caelynn shrugs. "This place does seem to have a strange effect on me. But no, I don't think it's the Night Bringer. His magic is mine. I'm confident of that. I completed his bargain, and part of that deal was the magic being entirely under my control."

I nod. "That's good. As long as you're sure."

"I'm sure. I remember what it felt like before I had control of it." She shakes her head. "It's mine now."

"Okay," I mutter and let the subject drop. I'm pleased she's confident the Night Bringer isn't messing with her from the inside out, but that doesn't change the issue that she isn't coping as well as I'd hoped.

I try to leave her be for a while, but my attention keeps shifting to her corner of the cave.

She fidgets and picks at her fingers like she's just not entirely comfortable. A few minutes later, she's playing with her hair and changing positions again. She lays her head back against the stone and breaths heavily.

Eventually, she notices me watching and then wrinkles her nose and crosses her arms. "What?"

I smirk at her endearing defensiveness. "Nothing. I just like watching you."

For the smallest of instances, her eyes grow wide and her cheeks flush. She covers quickly, though, and rolls her eyes. "Yeah, whatever. Creeper. What are you really thinking?"

I press my lips into a thin line and consider my next words carefully. It's true that I do like watching her. It's bittersweet. But maybe being truthful is the better option. "I'm just concerned is all. Things with you have been off. You look tired and uncomfortable. I just want to make sure you're okay."

Caelynn nods slowly. "I feel pretty drained. I don't know."

She pulls her knees up to her chest and casts her eyes to the ground.

"Do you need to sleep? I can keep watch." We both know that wasn't the plan, but I'm not going to push her too far. If she needs to rest, we'll find a way to make it work.

"No," she whispers. "I don't want to sleep."

I narrow my eyes, examining her again. Something is wrong. If it's not the magic and she's not physically tired, maybe... maybe she's given up more than I thought. Maybe it's not the Night Bringer tearing at her with his magic, maybe it's a real depression.

My stomach churns.

"Come here," I whisper, fed up with all the wondering. With the fear of losing her. I need her here, now. And I don't want her at arm's length.

Her eyes flash, golden light flickering for only a moment. I imagine her, for the first time, as my bride. As my lifelong lover. As the mother of my children. It's such an incredible picture that I have to blink back tears.

"Let's just take what moments we can, okay?" I whisper as all the explanation I'll give to her for this change. I want her near me. I want her in my arms. I want to feel her warmth and her life.

"Okay," she whispers, leaning back into me.

I can't have all of that, but I can have moments. I can steal pieces here and there. She shifts closer to me, but it's not enough. I lean in and grip her waist, guiding her over toward me. She obliges, though her low eyebrows tell me she's confused. Still, she scoots closer. I guide her so that she's between my legs, her back to my chest. I wrap my arm over her torso and pull her in tightly, my chin resting on her shoulder.

It's not a sexual position. It's not passionate, but it is intimate.

Her breathing is deep and deliberate like she's trying to keep herself calm.

"Is it okay?" I whisper. A strand of her hair bounces with my breath.

"Yes." She adjusts, settling deeper into my arms.

The crackling of fire is faint in the distance, and the orange glow grows brighter. Soon, the calls of the dead begin.

Moans and groans and whoops swirl in the air around us long before we see any sign of them.

Caelynn's hand on my forearm clenches and her nails dig into my skin.

"Shh," I whisper. "Relax. Focus on the magic hiding us. We'll be fine."

She nods and relaxes her grip. I can't let go of the concern that her heart or soul is growing dimmer. That light I saw when I last healed her was so small. A tiny flame in a raging storm.

It wasn't long ago she promised not to leave me. But I suppose that doesn't mean she sees any hope for herself. Prior to Reahgan's attack, she implied living out the rest of her life in these lands wouldn't be so bad. She said she didn't have much to live for even outside these walls. I know that was an exaggeration, she had at least one friend outside of the fae world, but she was adamant there was no real future for her there.

But clearly, it's affecting her.

After a while, her breathing evens out, and her body grows heavy against mine. The magic around the cave mouth flickers, and I wince. Is something wrong? Should I talk to her, shake her?

Her body slumps deeper into mine, muscles relaxed, and a gentle snore escapes her lips. A quiet joy rouses in my chest. She's asleep. She fell asleep in my arms, and I can't even express or begin to explain how good it feels.

The rippling over the cave mouth drops completely, leaving only a still blackness. It means we are not protected at all. We are only hidden by the natural darkness and stone walls cocooning us. I keep my gaze sharp, watching for anything out of the ordinary.

We want to remain unnoticed as much as possible. I have the ability to protect us if a wraith came wandering in here. I could even keep them out with a wall of light.

The problem is, I can't fight them all. And the moment we're exposed, they'll all come charging. It's probably reckless to let her sleep at all. At the very least, we should wait until nearly dawn before we allow our shield to drop, then she could sleep the last hour or two of the night and a few into the morning, leaving us plenty of time in the day to make our move on the spell book.

But I don't dare rouse her. I justify my choice by the fact that I need her at full strength to fight by my side. Caelynn is impressively powerful and resilient and smart. She is a better ally than I could have hoped for.

I silently thank fate for the day she was thrust on me in the trials. I had no choice but to accept her. If it weren't for that, I'd never have gotten to know her. I may have even killed her without knowing the truth.

The orb would have shown me, though. Assuming I'd survived the maze trial.

I can't even imagine what that would have done to me —if I'd killed her like I'd wanted and then found out she was my mate.

It would have haunted me for the rest of my life. How?

Why? I don't think I could have come up with a reasonable answer, and certainly nothing close to the truth.

I take in a long breath. She is mine now. I didn't complete my goal of killing her. Instead, I got to know her and my life was flipped upside down.

And now, I have her in my arms.

Things, obviously, are not ideal, but there is no way I'd go back and change anything about the trials. Maybe afterward, but that's something else entirely.

Before my thoughts can go too far off the rails, I readjust my frame of mind to the now. Tomorrow, we could be done with this mission one way or another. Pass or fail. Live or die.

Moving quickly is likely our best course of action. Once we plan on crossing the fire, we should strike. Rush over the next obstacle—a swamp of unknown origin or purpose. Followed by a small forest, or maybe just a couple of trees, the map isn't all that clear. Lastly, the single mountain in the middle. The spell book is said to be hidden inside. If we can cross the fire wall and then rush over the swamp, through the trees, and climb up the mountain quickly, we may be able to reach the book before the Night Terror is even aware.

My right arm begins to tingle, growing uncomfortable and numb. My back is growing sorer as time passes. It's likely been an hour or two since she fell asleep. I shift awkwardly, not wanting to wake her but desperately needing to relieve my own discomfort.

Caelynn jerks in my arms. Dammit.

She leaps up, nearly knocking her head on the stone ceiling. She hisses and spins in a crouch with a feral expression. The shadow wall slams back into place over the cave mouth. "You let me sleep?"

I give her a guilty expression but then smile. "Sorry?" I shrug innocently.

"Don't you realize how dangerous that is?"

My eyes flick down over her body. *Stupid.*

Her breath catches, and I know I've been caught. Her pupils dilate. But as much as I was growing uncomfortable in that position, I am missing her touch already.

"We're just fine," I answer calmly.

"We're lucky."

"You can stay awake till dawn now. Then, sleep a few more hours before we set out."

She purses her lips. "I don't need to sleep."

"Obviously, you do. You'll need your strength for whatever comes tomorrow." I hold my hand out to her, offering her a place in my lap again. Her gaze darts down then back up, her cheeks flaming red in an instant. Another rush of joy flashes over me.

"It's comfortable this way, isn't it?" I ask, deflecting her embarrassment.

She clears her throat and turns her back to me, settling in, this time with her rear on my leg. "Mhmm," she mumbles.

I quite like this position too. I grip her waist tightly, fingers finding warm, smooth skin where her shirt rides up.

"It's your turn to sleep."

"All right," I answer, but my mind is on anything but sleep now. "Maybe I should lie down instead—"

She lays her head against mine like she's too exhausted

to keep it up. "Not yet," she whispers, sending delicious chills over my body. Her hand rests on my neck, and I close my eyes, working to control my emotions. "I like where I am."

I grip her thigh with one hand, squeezing tighter than I should, her waist with the other, and I focus on breathing.

She doesn't want you. She doesn't want this, I try to remind myself. She rejected me just hours ago...

But she hadn't actually responded.

She flinches every time we're remotely intimate, but I can see the tension in her body ease. She seeks out my touch; she lingers when it happens by accident.

Her breath is shaky as it releases. I'm aware of every place our bodies connect. Her ass on my thigh, her back on my chest, the inside of my arm achingly close to her chest.

She wiggles, shifting down so she's between my legs again.

My lips graze her ear. I need to get this out. I need to find out where I stand. Because I don't want to keep desiring something that will only cause her more pain. Except, I can't help but feel like I can make some of this better for her.

That holding her, touching her, kissing her could give her the hope of what could be. Because, against my better judgment, I'm beginning to think that.

I fully intend to find a way to get Caelynn out of this place. I plan to steal her away from this curse. And once we're out in the real world—well, I don't know what that will mean, but I can recognize my own feelings well enough to know that I will continue to want her once I'm back in my comfortable palace. Once I'm king. Once I have all the things I've been working toward, there will always be something missing if she isn't there in some capacity.

The people may never accept her as queen or even as a consort of the king. But... but that's a fight for another day.

Today, I need to save her. And maybe it's presumptuous for me to assume that intimacy with me could do that, but she's so cold, so lonely, so sad. I want her to feel good. I want...

I take in a long breath, preparing myself for this conversation. "I need to know something," I say, my voice weak, unsure. "I need to hear it."

"What?" she whispers through the darkness.

I press my lips to her shoulder and pause for only a moment. "I want to make this better for you, Cae. In any way I can. So, I want to know what it is you need."

"I—don't..." She stumbles over her words.

"I have to know if you want me to leave you be, or if you want me to pursue you. I have to know if you want me the way I want you."

I can feel her muscles tense at my words, her breath leaving her lungs. Then, her breath puffs back, faster than before.

"Sometimes," I continue softly, "I get the feeling being close to me is painful for you. So, if I'm only making it worse, I'll stop. I'll give you space. As much as it'll torture me, I'll do it." I swallow. "But I want to be very clear that every moment we're together I desire *more*. I want you in my arms. I want to..." I close my eyes, unsure how detailed I should get.

Her heart pounds through her back and to my chest.

"Tell me what you want," she whispers in a desperate plea, sending a jolt of desire through my body.

I pull her in tighter, one hand clenching the bare strip of skin at her midriff. The other slides up her inner thigh. I tense beneath her, fire burning through my veins.

Caelynn gasps and wiggles against me.

My hand abandons the sweet skin of her stomach and curls into her hair, gripping tightly. I pull her head to the side to give me open access to her neck. My teeth graze her skin, and she whimpers. I sweep my tongue up to her ear and take it between my teeth.

"Tell me," she demands breathlessly.

"I want to explore every inch of your body, Caelynn. I want all of you."

She moans in earnest now, and it's enough to send me spiraling.

"I want to make you feel good, in every possible way." *Mine. My mate.* "Tell me what you want, Caelynn."

19
CAELYNN

I want his hands to never leave my body.

I want every barrier stripped from between us. These clothes and my scars.

I want to feel his muscles beneath my fingers, tracing every sharp edge, tasting every soft corner.

I want to kiss him.

I want to bed him.

I want him to call my name. To never stop uttering it with that desperate tone.

I want him to drive me into insanity, where all I feel is pleasure. All I feel is him.

I want Prince Reveln of the Luminescent Court to come apart at my touch. I want him to worship me, to bow before me. And for me to return the favor.

I want him to make me forget my fear and guilt and pain.

I want his warmth and comfort and safety.

I want a mate, a lover, and friend to hold me, keep me, comfort me.

But those are things I will never get in the Schorched-lands. And I don't want to pretend.

I want it to be real, but it never will be.

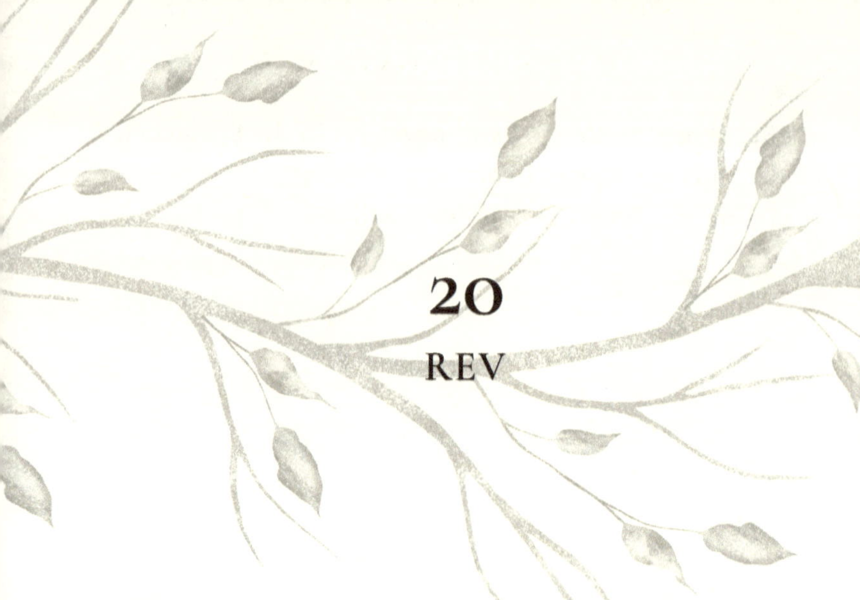

20
REV

"I want a lot of things, Rev," she whispers, her tone suddenly sober. "But not like this."

My veins cool in an instant. "Okay," I whisper and beg my heart to calm quickly.

My mind still spins over everything I want from my lovely shadow fae. I want to take her here, against the ash and dirt-covered stones of fae hell.

I want her any way I can have her.

But she's probably right. We haven't bathed properly in days. I don't even want to consider the filth we've had smeared on our bodies. We're in fae hell with evil just around the corner.

I slide my fingers from her hair and my hand on her thigh releases.

"Don't leave...Don't stop completely," she says. "Just..."

"Okay," I whisper again, understanding her. She wants closeness. She wants to feel me and know that I want her. But this isn't the time and place that she wants to bed me.

I open my mouth and graze sharp teeth against her soft skin. She shivers.

"Let me tell you one thing then," I say, lips just barely touching her. "When we get out of here... this—" I pause and run my nose over her neck. She squeezes my thigh. "This isn't over."

A soft moan escapes her lips, and that is the most beautiful sound I've ever heard. I vow to myself I'll hear it again. I will make her writhe with pleasure in a new way.

"One day," I mutter. "One day, I'll have you, Caelynn of the Shadow Court."

Caelynn chuckles. "Or perhaps it's me that will have you."

I let out a breath through my nose. "You can have me, Caelynn. I promise you that."

21

CAELYNN

My heart pounds so eagerly I can't think straight. Rev's hand settles back on my thigh, but its movement has halted. He doesn't slide it farther the way I'm secretly begging him to.

Every taste only makes me crave more. It's a never-ending cycle. I will never be satisfied.

Part of me is screaming for more. I want it. I need it.

But the other part is terrified.

I cannot have Rev. He isn't mine and hasn't been since the moment I shoved a dagger into his brother's chest.

You could have him now.

I press my eye together, willing back tears. I could have him for a moment. I could. And then be heartbroken when it's over. He talks like we'll both be free of this curse soon. Like he won't leave me behind in this place.

He talks like there will be more of us once we're out of here.

But I know better.

To be honest, that's another grace about my current circumstance. I won't ever live through that moment. Where Rev faces his real life and realizes what he had with me isn't worth losing it all.

He'll be king. And I could never be queen for many reasons. Some he doesn't even know yet. He'd take me as his for a night, a week—I don't know but not long—before he realized the truth. That there's no way for us to be together. We'll both be crushed if we take this much farther.

Logically, I know all of this. But his arms around me feel so good that I allow my mind to pretend. I won't settle for a rushed, haphazard moment of passion that's filled with bitterness. I won't allow myself to soil us in that way.

But in my mind, everything is right.

In my mind, he loves me. I am right for him. In my mind, all of the obstacles are gone, all of the what-ifs don't matter.

It is only him and me.

It is only his lips on my skin. His tongue exploring every inch.

I find myself wondering if his thoughts match mine. If we're here in this awful reality clinging to each other while simultaneously pushing away, but in our minds, we're together. In another world, another dimension, we're together. We're perfect.

My thoughts wind down because there is only so much I can do given my current circumstances. Eyes closed, I pretend to be lying in a big comfortable bed with silver covers and lush pillows, curled up in his arms. My cheek lies against his bare chest, my fingers curl into his over his torso that rises with calm, even breaths.

And we sleep. Just sleep, comfortable and safe, and together.

As much as I desire those other things, this is my perfect moment. Just being.

Whole.

Together.

Rev's grip on my thigh loosens over time. He shifts and huffs, his breathing evens, just like in my fantasy. Twisting my body to glance over my shoulder, I find his expression just as calm and relaxed as in my mind as well.

A small smile plays at my lips.

It's warm enough here we do not need a blanket. He has his blanket bunched up behind his head and his back-pack behind his back.

I scoot out and spread my own blanket down on the uneven ground beside him. Then, I grab his upper arms and guide him to lay down. He won't stay comfortable sitting up like that. He winces and groans but follows my guidance begrudgingly. I quickly grab his blanket and place it under her head just before he lays it down.

He settles into his new bed with a frown, his eyes still closed. Content with my handiwork I begin to move away from him when his fingers grip my wrist.

My heart sinks for an instant, but his eyes are still shut.

"Don't leave me, Cae," he mumbles.

I pull in a breath and hold it as my heart aches in the best way possible. "Okay," I whisper.

His hand falls limp to the ground, and I sit there

panting for a moment before finally taking my spot at the cave mouth, watching the dark valley below, and I wonder how the hell I got here. And what the hell it could possibly mean that Rev desperately wants to keep me with him.

22
REV

I force my dry eyes open, muscles stiff. The stone beneath me presses into my side uncomfortably. I'm surprised I'd been able to sleep like this at all.

The shiver of shadow magic covers us like a sheet, but there's no sign of my beautiful shadow fae ally.

Her smell, her touch, the sounds she makes pop into my mind all at once. I should be focusing on much more important issues—like survival—but she's stuck in my senses. I have to wait for anything more than these small pieces. I'll have to fight for her life, especially because I'm not convinced she'll fight for herself.

Her magic permeates the small space, so though I can't see her, and her backpack is missing I know she's near. I crawl toward the opening and pass through the shadow shield. Magic washes over me, sending chills over my whole body.

Only a few feet from the cave, a rock juts out over the edge of the mountain where we can get a decent vantage of the road leading to the fire wall. It's not as clear as the spot a hundred feet down the path, but I doubt Caelynn's magic would be so strong if she were that far away. The sky is still dark blue, but the edges of the horizon are lightening ever so slightly. Dawn is only an hour or two away.

I grab my backpack, still holding most of our supplies, just in case.

I climb up to the stone, which remains empty of life, and then in one instant, the misty darkness clears to expose a blond fae that takes my breath away. *God, she's beautiful.*

Her hair tosses in the wind, her eyes a dull bronze, which she narrows as she examines me.

"What?" I ask.

She pauses, leaning in ever so slightly. "What was that look?"

My lips part—I don't know. "I... was just thinking how beautiful you are." I shrug, my neck growing warm.

She frowns in confusion and closes her eyes like those words have affected her deeply.

Caelynn's eyes fly wide open, and then a rush of cold power washes over me. Her shadows curl around my back and grip me tightly, the darkness settling into my skin. I shiver. She motions for me to join her on the stone.

Together, we watch the pathway below as shadows shift. It's so dark I have a hard time making out all the forms, but there is certainly something down there. A group of wraiths, perhaps?

All I can make out are silhouettes of ghoulish figures as they move to and fro. The pathway here is fairly busy, but I wouldn't have expected this to be a central place of travel for the creatures in these lands. Hadn't we heard that not many wraiths travel past the wall? Why would they all gather under it?

A gentle rumble begins in the distance. My breath catches. Is it that beast again? A hush settles over the valley, the silhouettes below growing still. The entire valley seems to hold a collective breath.

What are they waiting on?

Another boom vibrates through us.

"Do you think..."

Caelynn grips my forearm tightly, and I cut my words off. Her pulse throbs against my arm, eyes focused below. Can she see more than I can? Probably. Shadow fae see in the dark significantly better than most other fae as a general rule.

The mountains surrounding us shudder, trembling like they, too, are terrified of the coming beast. The thundering footsteps grow louder, closer.

My heart is in my throat as the roaring flames crackle then split with a crack like lightning.

My heart is in my throat as a monolith silhouette appears in the dark flames. Caelynn's fingers dig deeper into my skin, and that's my only hint that she's also seen the creature.

"What is that?" I whisper.

The creature has to be fifty feet tall, with grey skin and red eyes. Black flames lick around its form where its skin still contacts the magical wall.

"Shh." Caelynn sits up ever so slightly.

I stumble in closer as her shadow shield tightens. Her dark magic brushes up against my skin, sending a wave of pleasure over my body.

The creature's chest and legs are as thick as trees, its skin nearly the same color as the mountains surrounding us, and massive black horns shoot from its skull and curl around its head.

The creature's eyes glow as red as the flames behind it. They turn our direction. Then, it takes another deliberate step, shaking the earth along with it.

The creature stands up straight on its hind legs. I swear this thing is half the size of the damn mountain.

"Is that her?" I whisper.

Caelynn groans in annoyance at my refusal to remain quiet, but if the Night Terror has just joined us in this part of the Schorchedlands, that's something I'd like to know. I suppose no matter who this creature is it can't be good. I'm just wondering what level of bad we're talking about.

The creature rumbles in what could be a laugh. As if this laugh was a signal, the wraiths restart their movement. Their groans grow into a thick wall of sound, surrounding us. Their smoke magic wafts through the hills and pathways below. And the creature just stands there.

For several minutes, we sit still as stone, cloaked by Caelynn's magic while the wraiths dance to the song of their own groans around the massive horned being. It's the weirdest thing I've ever seen.

"You shouldn't be here," a hushed voice—so much closer than the others—whispers through the wind, low and eerie.

I wince, and Caelynn sits up, a rusted iron knife in her grip. "What the hell are you doing here?" she hisses. "Haven't I made it clear you are not welcome with us?"

A being of dark smoke floats just feet above us. Caelynn's wraith.

"Telling you how foolish you are being, obviously."

"Last I heard, you didn't want to help us," I whisper. Either of us. It isn't just me he's working against now. Below, the tempo of the strange display hasn't changed. The wraith gathering hasn't seemed to have noticed our interaction.

"I have no desire to help you pass through the wall, no. But that is because I wish to keep your mate alive. Unlike you."

"I want to keep her alive too." My jaw clenches.

"I'll believe that when I see it. This is a very one-sided mate-ship, I will say."

My lip curls to expose my teeth, but Caelynn responds before I get the chance.

"It's not a mate-ship. No one has accepted or acted on anything. We are allies, doing what is best for each other."

My stomach twists, rejection bitter on my tongue.

The wraith chuckles, low and slow. "Neither of you believe that, do you?" He sighs dramatically and then spins around.

"What is this thing?" Caelynn asks quickly as if trying to change the subject or just get his attention before he leaves again. The wraith has made it very clear he's not my ally, but he does seem to want what's best for Caelynn. Perhaps in that way, we can be aligned—that is, when he's not trying to kill me. Half an ally is better than none, and he very likely has the information we require.

Perhaps it's time to turn the games on him so we can get what we need.

"A manticore." He waves his hand dismissively.

"It's not the Night Terror?" I ask.

The wraith pauses, facing me with eyes wide, and then blurts out in a hysterical laugh. "You think that is the Night Terror? Oh, dear boy, are you in for a surprise."

"I know it's not her. But what is it doing?" Caelynn asks.

My fingers curl on her waist gripping her tightly.

"It's a messenger, of course."

"A messenger?" I repeat.

"How else do you think she communicates with the wraiths on the outskirts?" The wraith's voice slurs and rumbles like the other moans wafting through the air. Is he trying to blend in? "Most wraiths refuse to pass the wall of flames, and she cannot. Not without sacrificing much of her power. So, her beasty does the crossing to pass along her orders and give gifts to those who obey."

"That thing isn't too evil to pass the flames?" Caelynn asks.

The wraith rolls his eyes. "That thing has no soul. And so, it cannot be affected."

I narrow my eyes. No soul. Do those animals have souls? Is that why the rabbits can hop through without so much as blinking?

"You said he gives gifts. What kind of gifts do wraiths desire?" Caelynn asks.

"The Night Terror can give the wraiths what many—

including you, if I remember correctly— have desired. To die content, clinging to the things they loved most. It's an illusion much like the Forest of Desires, but a strong one, and without the pesky issue of being eaten and tortured by trees. They will leave this world without pain. She also offers influence on the human world occasionally."

"They can influence the human world?" I mutter.

"Indeed. The Night Bringer is quite adept at that. Being ancient mated-beings, they can communicate. He knows all about what's happening with you, deary. You can be sure about that. And she has followed your journey closely all these years."

Caelynn tenses.

I blink slowly. I don't even want to know more. "So, what is it doing now?" I nod to the manticore.

"Nothing in particular. Making its presence known. Reminding his constituents of what they stand to lose if they fail. Perhaps gathering information."

"Information," Caelynn mutters. "On us."

The wraith tips his head forward, smoke billowing from his skull. "Yes."

Not altogether surprising. We've known they've been watching us since we left the cottage yesterday morning, but it's still unnerving. The bigger question is how much information have they been able to uncover?

"It knows we're here," Caelynn whispers.

I jerk my attention down to the manticore, whose red eyes look straight up at us. I lean in closer to Caelynn, lips grazing her ear. I'd like to appreciate the moment longer, but the panic rushing through my veins has me distracted. If that thing is simply the Night Terror's errand boy... I shiver. What *are* these creatures we've somehow become enemies of?

"Should we run?" I ask as quietly as possible. If we have that thing's attention…

Caelynn's wraith soars in front of us, blocking our view of the creature and his view of us.

The ground rumbles with the manticore's laughter. "You are but a pestering fly standing between me and my meal."

My blood runs cold at the sound of the creature's echoing voice. Caelynn's fingers tense on my knee.

"Don't worry, Shadowspell. Your time has not yet come. You may still be useful."

I can't see the creature now, but I can certainly hear his shuddering steps as he turns and the roaring of the flames as he steps back through them. wraith twists away with just enough time for me to see the flames close and resettle behind the massive beast.

I let out a breath as the fire licks and crackles just as before.

That monster saw us and turned around, leaving us alone.

These wraiths, thousands of them, flutter around the open air of the valley between the mountains. They answer to the Night Terror yet they do not act. What in the world could that mean?

"The Night Terror knows where we are. Why don't the wraiths attack us?" I ask.

"They have been ordered to give information only. But that doesn't mean they won't kill you if you're not careful. Keep that shield tight, Caelynn darling. Most of these wraiths are mindless. Every move, every choice, is based on instinct. Even with an order from the Night Terror to stand down, they will kill you if you make the wrong move. They desire your death. Each and every one."

"How about you?" I ask. Is he so different?

The wraith rolls his eyes. "I have my mind and soul entirely under my own control, thank you very much. Unlike most wraiths, I can choose."

"But you do desire his death," Caelynn nods toward me, her eyes lidded. A challenge.

"Desire is not the right word, child. I do not relish death. Nor do I wish to cause you pain. But if you refuse to take your place outside these walls..."

"Then, you'll kill me." I shrug. He wants me dead to save Caelynn.

The wraith sighs and twists awkwardly. "I will not kill you so long as she is safe. Does that make you feel better?"

Caelynn rolls her eyes. "Sure," she says. "A step in the right direction. How about if he's in mortal danger? Will you help him?"

"Absolutely not."

Caelynn throws up her hands.

The gathering of wraiths below begins buzzing anew, like an agitated swarm of wasps. Their moans rise in pitch. I swallow as I watch them. Light is on the horizon now. It's time for them to settle and find their hiding place for the day.

"Don't you see?" the wraith whispers, his voice full of desperation. "You cannot stand against them. You cannot defeat these wraiths, let alone the manticore, let alone the

Night Terror. It is an impossible task. Every moment you spend here, you increase their likelihood of escape.

"You must leave, Caelynn. You are the key to their schemes. If you remain out of reach, you can still achieve your goals. If you stay, if you pass through those flames, you will be in their clutches, and you will doom the world."

23
CAELYNN

Oh, wonderful. The fate of the world depends on me abandoning my soulmate in fae hell. Surprise, surprise.

"I don't trust you," I tell the wraith. I know what he wants, and he doesn't care about the fate of the world. He doesn't care about the plague. I wonder if he'd even care if it passed through the Shadow Court villages, killing all the children and taking away the elemental magic of our homeland.

I don't know. I don't care.

Because I know he is too selfish to make a proper choice. He has information I require, and that's the only reason I've entertained him this long.

"Leave us be," I tell him. "Your opinion is not needed."

The wraith's chest puffs up, and I cross my arms. He screws up his lips, but then his eyes turn to Rev. "Let her leave. Make her," he begs Rev, his words pointed, harsh. "It's the only way. If you love her, if you are any kind of mate at all, you'd choose her. You'd push her out and stay here in her stead."

Rage triggers in my chest, sparking an inferno of power inside of me. My vision turns back.

Kill him. Destroy.

Yes, I will kill him for daring to turn my mate against me.

An explosion of dark, acidic power blasts from my body, ripping at every seam. I roar in rage as I leap at the wraith. "Get out of here!"

I can't think. I can't see anything but the wraith that called himself my ally. That claims to be my ancestor. That wants to turn my mate against me. That wants to kill him.

The nameless wraith, one of my few allies, slams into the stones across the valley.

I send another blast, larger than the last, filled with my rage and terror.

Hissing halts below us. Silence settles in the valley, another held breath.

Hundreds of wraith eyes, void but eager, turn toward us.

"No," my wraith whispers. "What have you done?"

I bare my teeth at him, preparing for another attack, but then warmth presses into my back. Strong but gentle arms wrap around me and pull me back. My muscles sag into them. My mind spins, a mixture of confusingly conflicting feelings. Anger but comfort. Hate but love. Frigid agony but warm hope.

Pressure digs into my skin at my waist. Fingers, I realize.

Nausea sweeps over me as I force my magic back down

and give in to my mate. He cocoons me, protects me, holds me.

"Shh, Caelynn." His voice murmurs in my ear, and my eyelids flutter.

Rev.

Mine.

I pant, barely registering what's happening, but I don't fight him.

"Stop, Caelynn." It's the fear in his voice more than anything else that brings my consciousness back to the forefront. The rising groans of the dead bombard me in an instant. Their forms swarm and twist into a wave of toxic magic. The decaying souls of the wraiths in the valley have shifted their sights on Rev and me. They murmur eagerly.

"Kill."

"Devour."

"Little children have come to die."

"Rev." My voice shakes. "I'm sorry," I breathe. I lost control, lost my mind. My magic that was supposed to protect us has doomed us.

The wraiths are coming. And unlike the manticore, they do not intend to let us go.

24
REV

I hold onto Caelynn tightly, praying we can somehow make it out of this alive. A swarm of wraiths buzz below. They call to us.

"*Kill,*" they cry.

"*Take them.*"

"*Rip them apart.*"

Their moans are desperate and eager, leaving the hair on my forearms standing up straight. Caelynn falls nearly limp in my arms. Is she okay? Is her mind under her control?

I knew I had to stop her, for both of our sakes, but something snapped inside of me too. Enough to understand her reaction. I remained calm, but my magic flared white-hot, desperate to reach her, desperate to save her from herself.

The wraith became both of our enemies at that moment.

He's disappeared into the shadows now. Perhaps realizing there is no hope of escape for us. He can't stop an army of wraiths this large any more than we can.

My teeth chatter. I'm thankful Caelynn has seemed to get herself under control, but terrified of the shift in calls from the wraiths below. I lean back just enough to meet Caelynn's dark eyes.

"I'm sorry," she whispers.

"What do we do?" I ask, breathlessly. "Can you hide us?" My voice cracks as I ask Caelynn the only thing I could imagine may help us. I don't even know if she's capable now.

"It won't matter." She whimpers. "We can't hide from them now."

I wince at her answer, but determination solidifies in my chest. It might be hopeless, but I won't give up.

Only one possible action remains. Run.

I pull Caelynn by the waist and together we sprint down the pathway, away from the fire wall, just as the swarm of wraiths reaches our camp. My feet pound on the gravel as fast as they can carry us.

Roaring pain carves through my back as a wraith's magical claws slice through my jacket reaching the soft flesh below. I stumble. Caelynn snarls, holding me up with one arm while the other blasts an arrow of shadow magic at my attacker.

A dark puff of magic bounces off of him, sending him bounding into three wraiths behind him. *Only a few thousand left to go.*

"Can we get to the cabin?" I ask.

"That magic won't save us this time, Rev."

I know she's right the moment the words leave her

mouth. Is there any hope? Is this it? Is there really no way to get out of this?

"The fire wall." Caelynn pants, sprinting beside me. "They won't cross it."

My heart rises and then sinks immediately. "You mean the fire wall we're running away from?"

She doesn't respond, and I don't blame her. A half-baked plan forms in my mind, but it's enough to spark the hope I desperately need to keep running, to push harder. These wraiths are mindless, as Caelynn's wraith told us.

If we curl all the way around the mountain with them trailing, it may leave our path open to reach the wall. If we can make it that far.

The swarm of wraiths is just behind us, nipping at our heels.

We are on one of the smaller mountains… Maybe we can make it. I don't have the breath or presence of mind to explain my plan, but she keeps up with me step for step.

"*Come to us,*" the wraiths cry in unison.

"*Come to die.*"

"*Join us. Become like us.*"

The voices surround us, curling in, eerily bouncing off of the mountains—so much I can't tell which direction they're coming from. I can only hope they're still behind us or this plan is fruitless.

Our pathway ends abruptly, but we don't have time to think or seek a new path. We leap over the edge, falling through the shadows below.

We crash down onto solid ground. I stumble, but Caelynn pulls me up and propels me forward. We are in a pass on the west side of our mountain. The sky is bright red over its black silhouette. Sharp slabs of stone cover either side of our narrow passageway. We've got to pray it leads all the way through because if not, we'll be trapped.

My legs ache. My lungs burn. But I flee for my life—and Caelynn's. I hold her hand tightly in mine, praying she won't try to sacrifice herself to free me.

I can't lose her now.

I won't.

We barely remain ahead of the herd for a full mile, and the heat begins to increase. The sky grows redder, glowing. We're close. So close.

The pathway curls back around, opening to the roadway.

The firewall comes into view, its intimidating, roaring flames hundreds of feet up. It's raging heat burning hot on my skin. Its stacks of black smoke waft into the sky. It's less than a mile away now, we can make it. We can—

Black smoke wings flash in front of us, and we both slide to a stop. I blast light at the wraith, and it screeches, flying in the opposite direction. But my hand flies to my mouth as a swarm of wraiths drop in front of us. They twist and spin together, creating a wall, rising in the sky, blocking our path.

"Fuck," Caelynn hisses. Another wall of wraiths forms behind us.

I grip Caelynn's hand, panting desperately. My magic is nearly full, though I suspect Caelynn can't say the same. I can fight. I can probably blast through a set of them and maybe get us through... maybe. I pull in my magic, charging the heat, gathering it to fight for me.

The wraiths shift, each one moving to the right,

forming a spinning circle around us. The wind picks up as their speed does.

"Come to die, children," they moan.

They move so quickly around us that soon, they blur together and the wind rips at our clothes.

"They're making a fucking wraith-magic tornado," Caelynn shrieks. "What the fuck?"

I pull her in closer, arms wrapping around her waist. She melts into me. There's no escape now. They have us surrounded on every side. She presses her face into my neck. I realize this might be our last moment alive.

A rush of ice-cold magic overwhelms me for one quick instant, and I yell out in surprise. Caelynn clenches my arms, fingers digging into my skin. Her eyes are pressed closed in concentration.

"What are you doing?" I call over the roar of the raging storm.

The dump of glacial magic bombards me again, only, this time, I recognize it as shadow magic.

"Caelynn!" I cry out.

She doesn't respond. Is this another one of her episodes? Has she blacked out again?

The raging storm of wraith magic surrounds us on every side. They made a tornado out of their joint magic, and we are at the center of it. The center, which is closing very quickly.

The blur of black wind sweeps toward us in one massive surge. The roaring winds rip at our clothing. My bag flies into the storm, all of our supplies lost. I desperately grip my pocket to make sure I haven't lost my precious stone. It warms in my pocket—or is that just my imagination?

One last surge and the brunt of the storm slams into my back, ripping through my flesh.

I scream as chaos takes over every sense. There is pain and magic and chaos and—her. Caelynn's intense grip on my forearms barely keeps me grounded. My feet release from the ground, claws digging into my shoulder, ripping. Caelynn cries out, though I don't even know how I could hear her in the thundering roars of the dead, but it's inside of me. Her pain. My pain.

Our pain.

Her scream echoes through the tornado of wraiths, gripping me, burning, searing. I thrust a wall of luminescent magic around us and their magic falters. We fall back to the ground in a heap of limbs. I can do that again and again, but eventually, I'll run out of magic and they won't. There are too many of them.

And there is nowhere to run.

The roaring wall of wind crashes into us again, and Caelynn leaps toward me as she latches her arms around my body, and that cold shadow magic grips me again.

I'm torn apart. My skin splitting. I'm certain death has me in its grip when even my mind is split, giving way to the void of dark shadows.

25
CAELYNN

I knew I would die today, here in the Schorchedlands.

But of all the ways I expected it to happen—a wraith-nado was not on my list of possibilities. Death by wraith? Hell yeah. Being ripped to shreds by thousands of them at once while they used their magic to mimic a natural weather pattern?

Not so much.

I dig into Rev's arms, knowing I could be doing serious damage, but letting him go is not an option. Torn muscle and shards of fingernail broken inside his flesh are significantly better than death.

All I can think is that I cannot let him go. *Hold on. Hold on. Hold on.*

All of it, everything I've ever sacrificed, was for him. It will not end this way. I will not give up on him so long as I have breath in my lungs.

Love or hate. Adoration or disgust. Hope or pain. I don't care about any of it.

He will live. I will not. Those are the facts I know without a doubt.

And so, even though I've used too much of my magic already, I pull at every ounce to save him.

Save him. Save him.

Mine, my magic whispers in response.

Yes! He is mine. Take him with us!

My magic whips out, wraps around my mate, tearing at his very being until he is no more.

———

My back slams into the thick hot mud. Rev's chest slams into mine, taking away my breath—and not in a good way.

His eyes are wide as a wraith's empty sockets as he stares at me. The wind is gone—or rather, it's a hundred feet north of us at the moment.

My vision blinks black, and Rev rolls off of me.

I suck in desperate breaths. My limbs tingle, bare of magic.

This is not the place to be stuck without magic. But then again, it doesn't matter if I die. It's probably better that way.

The wall of flames flickers just a few feet away, heat like an oven rolling off of it, burning my skin. I'll pass out if we stay this close to it for too long.

Anxiety crawls through me at the thought of walking into that. But we have to.

"What just happened?" Rev asks, and I shudder out another breath.

It worked. That's the only thing I can think of. It actually worked. I swallow and turn to the flames. "We have to go in," I say, terror clinging to my limbs. I'm petrified of this magical fortress. And I'm horrified of what lies on the other side.

The roaring winds of wraith magic still overpower most sounds. The tornado rages just a few dozen feet from where we stand, but they've have not yet realized we escaped their trap. They rip our supplies and my lost jacket to shreds, but I have to assume that it won't take them long to figure out that their prey has escaped. And we did not make it far.

One shift, one moment, and they'll have us in their grasp again.

"What did you do?" Rev says, brushing the hair from my eyes. "How?"

I swallow. "I don't know."

I don't know how it's possible for me to shadow-walk him along with me. It's not supposed to be possible. But since I'd somehow been able to shield him with my magic when that had formerly been impossible, I knew I had to try.

"Are you okay?" he asks, gently gripping the ends of a strip of hair. His magic flashes in this palm then fades, almost as if he can't control it.

"Fine," I lie.

He narrows his eyes. His magic flashes again, this time rushing into my chest. I convulse with the shock, but the tingling is gone, my magic squirming beneath the surface. Did he... just give me some of his magic?

"What the hell was that?"

He smirks. "I don't know."

A series of high-pitched shrieks behind us makes me jump. "We have to go."

He turns to face the wall of flames, probably realizing the same thing.

This very well may burn us alive, leaving only dust in its wake. Only one of us may make it to the other side. Maybe neither of us. But we have to go.

His cheeks are flushed with heat. "Together," he says, with a determined gait. He clenches his jaw tightly, and I nod. Tears well in my eyes.

It's pathetic how afraid I am. Of all of it.

Of what it might mean that we can exchange magic the way we have.

Of losing Rev. Of loving Rev. Of the look in his eyes that tells me he might love me too.

I'm afraid of burning. I'm afraid of judgment. I'm afraid of what's waiting on the other side.

This moment is the epitome of it all, and I don't know if I could do it alone. But Rev steps closer, his fingertips gently drift up to my cheek until he cups it. Chaos and terror are inches away, but for this one moment, we're back in the Luminescent Court ballroom. We're young and naïve. Unscarred.

We have hope.

This one moment, his silver eyes meet my gold ones and we are just us.

When he leans in, his lips press to mine so slowly, so gently, the world fades away. All my fear. All my anger. All my pain. It's all gone.

All that's left is Rev. He steps back towards the flames, hand outstretched, waiting for me to join him.

I'd follow him anywhere. Even into the very flames of judgment.

I pause for one last moment to appreciate his beauty, the pulsing red of the furnace behind him. Then, I grip his neck and tug his lips to mine one last time.

And before our kiss ends, I grip his shirt and pull him with me into the raging inferno.

Because if my whole world is going to implode, this is how I want it all to end.

26

REV

Caelynn clings to me as we fall together into the flames.

Scorching agony explodes over every sense. The intensity overwhelms me as it burns from the inside out. But... it's not exactly pain. Not in a physical way.

My soul explodes with flashes of feelings and memories. My lovely court of reflecting light. My brother taunting me as a child but then extending his hand to help me. My father hitting my mother as she clings to me. Shielding me.

Then, it shifts to *her*.

Caelynn's golden eyes, soft and beautiful. Her blond hair loose with wild curls. Her smile is full of mischief. She's young and bold but innocent. So impossibly beautiful.

My mate, my soul whispers.

Then, an onyx black talon the size of my forearm emerges from her chest, carving through her body and spouting black blood. Her expression crumples in terrible pain. When she screams, so do I.

The images shift to my brother's funeral. Despair washes over me. My heart breaks all over again.

Then I'm back at the Flicker Court ballroom, at the beginning of the trials. When she boldly entered the hall. This time, when I see her march down the aisle—as stares filled with hatred like daggers, sneers, and whispers cascade over the room—I see what I missed before.

I hated her more than all the rest. And yet, now, as I'm shown the scene again, I see her pain. She was so lonely. So sad. So guilt-ridden.

And when I shoved her down. When I threatened her...

She stood still and stoic. She held it all in. But I can't. Regret strangles me. Black blood, like that which splattered from her when that monster carved into her, fills my lungs until I'm choking for breath. I claw at my chest, trying to break free from the guilt. Free from the pressure suffocating me.

Caelynn.

Forgive me.

———

I fall to my knees on slick mud, gasping for air. I press my forehead to the ground, hot liquid dampening my hair. The wall of flames flickers beside me, but the air is cooler. Still warm but not an oven-like before.

My breaths are labored, my mind spinning, my body

aching, but I take a moment to wrap my mind around the fact that I made it through.

A hundred feet beyond the flames is a bank covered in shiny black stones and a steaming swamp beyond it. In the distance, one mountain stands alone. The center of it all.

Next to the mountain is a massive tree with leafless branches reaching to the sky like worshiping hands.

The wall of flames showed me only what I already knew. That my whole life was centered around Caelynn. All of it was for her and because of her. I didn't even get through all of it, only pieces of our journey together. But it was enough to drown me in guilt.

Yet, somehow, I made it through the judgment.

Caelynn, my soul still calls for her.

"Caelynn," I force out through my raw throat. I made it to the other side of the flames, my soul beaten and battered but whole.

But my lips are cold. My hands, that held her tightly just moments before are empty.

"Caelynn!" I scream. I spin, looking for her. *No.*

No. She can't be gone.

I can't lose her now. Not like this.

I wait, moments stretching out into infinity—eternity without her. It will destroy me, suffocate me.

I can't.

My soul rips at the thought that she could possibly be gone. I pull myself onto wobbly feet and stare at the flame, preparing to reenter the magical wall—even if it means facing the wraiths on the other side. I'm not giving up on her. Not now.

"What did you do?" A deep and furious voice rumbles behind me.

I blink back tears, my chest tight, and I turn to find the black wraith staring at me, dumbstruck. Caelynn's ancestor that wants her to live and me to die. His face is contorted with rage.

"Caelynn," is all I can manage to force out. I point toward the wall of flame.

His billowing smoke pops and crackles like a fire. "You..." he accuses. "You've destroyed her. Over and over." His eyes flash red. "And you would *dare* to lose her now? Like *this*?" he screams, and when he flies at me, I barely have the strength to fight back.

27
CAELYNN

Fire quakes around me as it takes hold of my body. Everything else falls away until there are only roaring red flames tearing into my soul.

I arch my back, hair flying as pain explodes behind my eyes.

Memories bombard me, but they flash so fast I can barely register them. All the things I once wanted but were taken from me. Things I'd let go of so long ago.

My vision turns entirely black. I blink, but I can't tell the difference. There is no sound. Silence isn't a strong enough of a word to define it. I can't hear or feel my own breath.

Am I... alive? I can't tell.

The tiniest of lights glow softly in the distance. I move toward it, though I'm not certain if I'm stepping. Do I even have a body? I can't feel it. I can't feel anything at all.

The little flame, smaller than a match's light, flickers. Darkness presses in on it. The wind begins to blow—the first sound I've heard since... I don't know when. Since I've been here? Wherever here is.

The wind picks up speed, whipping at the tiny helpless flame. My heart aches, somehow knowing this flame is important.

I pity the little thing. There's no way it can survive this storm.

I blink, and there are hands surrounding the flame. Large hands with rough skin and a scar along one thumb. He's saving the flame or trying, at least. Protecting it from the raging storm.

"Why bother?" I mutter. It's hopeless.

The protector's eyes flash to me, angry. He snarls, silver eyes darkening.

I turn from the faltering flame and continue through the enteral darkness.

My heart sinks as something shifts in the blanket of darkness before me. The nothingness ripples.

Then, I see him.

A being so massive he's like darkness incarnate. All around. Inside of me. Controlling me.

Night Bringer.

No, I scream inside, but I can't move. I'm frozen.

He laughs as he sends slashes of wind through the air. I wince at the attack, but it simply blows my hair back and continues slicing through the air past me, straight to the figure protecting the little flame.

This last strike puffs out the flame like a breath, here then gone.

The Night Bringer roars in triumph, laughing hysterically. Except it doesn't come from the darkness before me. It comes *from* me.

My lips move. "You've lost, my pet," I say with his voice. "My *host*."

The floor falls out from beneath me, and I fall through pitch blackness clawing at me. Fall. And fall.

My choice, my hope, my innocence, my *very soul* stolen from me. Ripped away. So easily discarded.

No, a harsh voice booms through the darkness. My body slams onto hard smooth ground, my vision still only seeing a blanket of pitch-black covering everything.

The blanket of blackness flickers, revealing searing red flames. *Never your soul.* The deep, strangely familiar voice echoes through me.

Suddenly free from the raging pain, I open my eyes. All I see are flames flickering and reaching for me.

"What?" I ask the voice.

My mind is free from the spell for a moment.

He took many things from you, child. But your soul was never one of them.

I pull in a long breath. "Who are you?" I ask stupidly. Is this part of the trial? Part of the magic of the flames? It feels... foreign. Like something else is here, pushing me along.

"I am the keeper of the magic of these lands. My very being is stitched into every ounce. It is my punishment. My eternal prison."

I blink as it suddenly clicks. I do remember the strange feminine voice.

"The Wicked Gates," I mutter.

"Yes, I am the keeper of the gates."

"Did I pass my judgment?" I blink, thinking of the extinguished flame. "Did I fail?"

Is that why everything was black, why she's talking to me now?

"You are not yet finished, Caelynn of the Shadow Court. But I do have a message for you."

I look around, the flames flicker near me, but they don't touch my skin. I don't see any sign of anyone else. No Rev, no other form. Does this... being have no physical form?

"What is the message?" I ask, curious more than anything else.

"Well, first, that that monster did not, could not, touch your soul."

I pull in a breath.

"You've always believed it. He led you to believe it. That he somehow damaged you so deeply that there was no recovering from the assault. Only you can destroy your own soul, child. If he'd stolen your soul, killed it like you believed, you would have killed Reveln that first time you met him. You would have felt no regret. You'd have been the perfect puppet. No, Caelynn, you have always been so much more than that. And you have to learn to forgive yourself for what was outside of your control."

"I don't understand... why would you be telling me this? Why..."

"Why would the Wicked Gate, the magic of punishing lands, care about your soul?"

"Well, yes. Do you do this for all the souls who pass through here?"

"Yes. Though I admit, I am not quite as invested in every soul as I have become in yours."

Mine? "Why?"

"Because you have been unfairly placed in the center of a battle so much older and larger than yourself. You are, unfortunately, the pin at the center of it all. If you fail, we all fail. If you fall, the world will be at their mercy once again."

"Why?" I whisper. "I'm not that special."

"Well, that's certainly debatable, child. But you are right, that you are just a fae like any other. You were not born exceptionally powerful. And this burden should not be on your shoulders. But you are the one they chose, and that put you right in the center of it all."

Chosen. By those monsters. Because they believed me to be like them. They saw the darkness inside and…

"Stop, child. Ambition is not evil. It is not your desires that matter. It is *choice*. You already made it clear that the Night Bringer was wrong about you. You are better than him. So much stronger inside than he can even comprehend."

I swallow.

"It is by chance that you are here, that you are the center of it instead of so many before you. It is not fair to you. And yet, that will not change the truth. And so, you are the one we must rely on."

"So, what do I have to do?"

"Keep to the right path, Caelynn."

I blink. For a moment, I think she's going to tell me to go back home. Leave Rev here like my wraith wants.

"No, child. I would never expect one to abandon their mate. That would destroy your soul quicker than the depression your hopelessness has brought. Your ancestor is a wraith for a reason, child. His greatest flaw is his self-ishness. He will devour anything, trample anything, to achieve his goals. If he had known that chaining the Night Terror would dismantle his beloved court, he would have let the world fall."

"Then what? Am I to die?"

The gate pauses. "Seek the right death, Caelynn. Alive or dead does not matter so much as protecting your soul."

"I have one final vision for you before you continue on your journey. But this is my message. I am sorry for your pain. Sorry for this war you were thrust into. The innocence stolen from you. In order to win, you must protect your soul, Caelynn. Resist their darkness. You have the power, the strength to survive."

A rush of magic washes over me in an instant, and I no longer remember where or who I am. There is a surprising peace, a fluttering of hope and love.

The pressure, the weight, the burden—it's gone. Why was I so burdened before this moment? I cannot remember. I cannot even fathom. But I do know that this feels good.

Death is freedom, a whisper floats through my mind, and I blink rapidly. This whisper is heavy, so much heavier than the sprites.

No, another whisper floats by. *The right death, is freedom.*

Follow the right death, Caelynn.

28
REV

Caelynn's wraith's magic stings like acid as it slams against my body. His hands curl over my throat, and I choke back, trying to twist away, but I don't use my magic. Not a spark of the white light that could cast him off in only a moment.

The pressure over my head feels so complete I swear my brain is moments from exploding. Finally, light flickers over my palms, just enough to toss him to the side. He skids to a stop over the shimmering black pebbles. The smoke that makes up his body flickers. He bares his black teeth at me. "I will kill you. I should have killed you the moment I knew Caelynn would continue to choose you no matter what it cost her."

I press my hand over my throat, pressing tightly over the slick wound. It's pouring blood. *Wonderful.*

"You would let him kill you?" I whip my head at the new voice. Smooth and poised, it drifts from the trees beside the swamp.

The wraith and I both twist to face the forest as

another wraith approaches. His magic is light grey, eyes glowing silver. Reahgan always was powerful.

Despite the rage and doubt swirling in my chest now, I take in a long breath and close my eyes, just long enough to pull in the magic I need to stop my bleeding. The blinding light from my palms causes both wraiths to jerk back, covering their eyes.

"Yes, use up all that magic of yours. You'll be easier to kill."

"You will not touch my brother," Reahgan says, each word pointed.

"If Caelynn is already dead—" I pause, heart-clenching at those words. "Why does it matter now?"

And if Reahgan, who's entire plan centered around her death, is here, does that mean he had a part to play in her demise?

The shadow wraith's face falls. "I...." His jaw sets, eyes determined but sad. "I do not know for sure she is gone."

Reahgan chuckles, but my breath shudders. "What are the chances?"

My eyes flash to the burning flame behind us. There is no commotion. No hint there is anything happening inside. There's just... nothing.

"She is not dead, dear brother. But she may soon wish she was."

I wince as a blade—or something just as sharp— presses tightly against the underside of my jaw. I freeze, every muscle tense.

"Do not move, rodent," a voice deeper than I'd ever heard growls at me, and my vision wavers in panic.

Reahgan crosses his arms confidently.

What have you done? I think but don't dare mutter a word.

Because whatever has a hold of me now... it is much worse than a wraith.

29
CAELYNN

Wet ground squishes beneath my fingers, against my cheek. I groan and push myself up. My muscles scream in protest, and I let out a trembling breath.

"Ow," I say, sitting upright. I press my palm against the side of my throbbing head. "What the hell?"

After a few deep breaths, I manage to do a sweep of my surroundings. In front of me is the vicious fire, but the air is several degrees cooler than before. The ground is mushy dirt. The edge of a murky swamp sits only a few feet behind me. There is a small forest to my left and open water to my right. In the center of the murky water are stones spread over the length like a pathway.

My brain is still overloaded, my body still throbbing in pain, but I force myself to think things through. We were attacked by wraiths and somehow made it through the fire. We... *Rev.*

My breath catches. He should be here. I stand on wobbly feet, my heart pounding in my head. "Rev!"

Nothing. It's so quiet here. So still. The sky is hazy red. How long had I been in the flames? It was just shy of dawn when we entered. Now, Rev is gone and it's as bright as the sky gets in the Schorchedlands.

Behind the wall of flame, I know, is an army of wraiths seeking to rips us apart.

My hands shake. Did Rev not make it past the fire? *No,* how could he have failed that judgment? It's me that has the soiled soul. He's... well, he's not perfect, but he's good. Better than me.

"Rev!" I call again, louder. I know it's a risk. I know it's stupid given my circumstances. The wolf told us there was an ambush waiting on the other side of the flames. I know there were thousands of wraiths beyond the fire—how many of them would cross to find me here? At least a few, I'm guessing. And my magic is not exactly at full strength, even with Rev's help.

And how far off is the Night Terror? She could be anywhere.

God, I need to find Rev.

"Ahh," a voice calls joyously. "The princess decides to grace us with her presence."

My wraith drifts over, his smoky magic billowing side to side like a dance. His body language is all casual. His expression is... odd.

"Wonderful," I mutter under my breath.

"What's wrong, lovely daughter of mine?" He smiles, big and obnoxious.

"Stop. Where is Rev?" I spit at him. "Have you seen him?"

"Ahh. So, you do not want to entertain my presence...

until you want something from me? How is it that you living-beings are so ignorant all the time? How do you live that way?"

I stand and wipe the muck from my leather pants. "You're damn right. I don't trust you, so I don't want you around me. But if you have information, I'll take it."

He heaves in a dramatic breath, placing his clawed hand over his chest. "And what, dare I ask, makes you think I would give you the information you seek?" His smile is cruel and amused as he leans in to peer into my eyes.

"I expect nothing from you," I say. "Except perhaps to point me in the directionless likely to end in my death."

He tsks at me. "Stubborn, stubborn child."

I step toward the edge of the water barely moving with a tiny current, rustling up over the smooth black stones peppering the bank, glistening and lovely. I expected something awful here. I expected a war zone smothered with dead bodies and blood and poison. Not something beautiful and peaceful.

"Where is Rev?" I ask the wraith again. "Did he pass through the fire? Is he alive?"

"Yes," he hisses.

I let out a long breath, trying to keep my mind calm. Okay, that's good, I guess.

"Then, where is he?" I examine the area. Is he hiding somewhere, waiting for me? Did something happen?

The body of water between me and the mountain, where darkness gathers and smoke billows, is smooth and calm. No sign of a fight. No sign of Rev.

My stomach sinks even further.

The wraith purses his lips and floats around me. "You took longer to pass through. He didn't think you made it. He moved on without you." He shrugs as if that's all there is to it. As if this news wouldn't crush me.

My breath catches in my throat. "He thinks I'm dead?"

The wraith nods. Why does that hurt so badly? It's what we both expected. It's what probably should have happened.

Protect your soul.

I close my eyes and shake my head, unsure what to think.

Rev... moved on without me.

My fingers run along my bottom lip, where just minutes ago his soft lips met mine. I'd thought it meant something. As much as I knew I couldn't fall for him without getting crushed all over again, some reckless part of me did anyway.

My shattered heart crumbles even more.

I blink rapidly, trying to wrap my mind around it. He's out there, somewhere, looking for the spell book. There's no sign of him, which means he's already passed the swamp entirely.

"He was distraught over your demise, of course," the wraith adds sympathetically. "But he still has a quest to complete."

I ignore that comment. "How long did it take me to pass through the fire?"

The wraith shrugs. "A quarter of an hour, I'd guess."

Fifteen minutes. In fifteen minutes, Rev gave up on me and continued alone?

Between the pain in my chest and the dizziness, I narrow my eyes at the wraith.

"Where did he go?" The words come out in a pathetic whisper.

"Through the swamps, toward the book, of course."

Stones crunch beneath my feet. Tiny, shiny black pebbles scattered across the whole bank like a black beach. This is certainly the loveliest sight I've yet seen in this dark place. If I touch the shining black stones, will they splatter into blood? Or will they come to life and attack me like creepy little spiders?

I swallow, hyper-focusing on the lovely stones. Anything to avoid the reality that I'm alone. Again. *He left me behind.*

My heart and mind are numb, and I'll keep it that way as long as I can manage. Just a little while longer and I can wallow in my pain.

I eye the little stones the way around the water, as far as I can see. "What are these?" I ask the wraith, gentler than before. I'm alone, Rev is nowhere to be seen, and he is the only ally I have now.

I don't have the energy to continue to push him away. Not now. Not until I find Rev.

"Soul stones," the wraith says quietly. "All that's left of every soul that has ended in this terrible place."

I purse my lips. "They're beautiful. Are they... dangerous?"

"No. Unlike every other aspect of this terrible place, those are exactly what they appear. Useless but lovely. A reminder of what was lost and can never be reclaimed."

My heart aches, heavy with loss. I don't even know

why. I don't know these souls, but there is a weight here, a sense of loss, hanging over everything.

"This was the original resting place for all magical souls that do not pass on. It predates the Schorchedlands by millennia."

Was there a time the Schorchedlands didn't exist? Technically, I know that must be true—I've spoken to the creators of the walls, heard about the animals trapped inside at the time of the curse—but the thought that an afterlife existed before the Schorchedlands isn't something I'd ever considered.

I squat down, examining the pebbles closer. Broken. Lost. But no longer afraid. Why am I so enamored by the little stones? Perhaps it's because their fate will soon be mine.

Time is ticking away. I should be searching for my lost mate... because even if he's moved on without me, he may still need my help. But my numb heart pounds slowly, my mind frozen on this one small aspect.

Souls of lost fae beneath my feet.

Something about this place draws me in. I want to lie beside the stones and join them in their final slumber. I finally risk a gentle touch of the stones piled on the bank of the smooth lake. They don't attack me. They don't hurt. They act as any other pebble. Smooth and pretty but lifeless.

Down the bank, at least fifteen feet away, a gentle white light flickers off of a stone. I narrow my eyes, moving toward the sight before I even decide to move. "What's that?"

The wraith turns and drifts along with me. "What is what, child?"

It's tiny, the little white gem hidden among the smooth black stones. I bend down and examine it before I dare touch it. I don't know why this little stone has caught my attention so deeply. Around me, the souls of millions of fae scatter across the bank. But this one is so very different.

It looks like a diamond almost, but it flickers light all around. It reminds me of Rev. Of the Luminescent Court and that forest of clear-leaved trees bouncing light everywhere.

I drop to my butt beside the rare stone and look out over the water. Deceivingly simple, this part of the Schorchedlands. Wetlands like any other—besides the general darkness and eternally leafless trees. I know without a doubt that there will be more to it.

I push the pain from my mind, and on a whim, I grip the white gem between my fingers. I don't want to leave it here for some reason.

The wraith's attention shifts to my fingers as I stand. "What is that?"

"I don't know," I admit. It could be worthless for all I know, but it's so out of place here in the Schorchedlands, even among the lovely soul stones.

He drifts closer, his eyes widening in horror. "Drop that, now!" he practically yells.

And yet, I don't. I won't. "Why?"

"Because it is not yours. It doesn't belong to you," he snarls.

Now, that has my attention. My mind sharpens. "What is it? You know where it came from?"

There is a gentle warmth radiating from the tiny stone, and it flickers light onto my palm.

"Yes," he hisses. "You must leave it behind."

I tilt my head, examining him. He's angry, not afraid. Does the stone mean something to him? "Tell me or I'm going to bring it along."

"It's..." He pauses. "It's from the Night Terror. It will tell her where you are at all times." He winces.

I raise my eyebrows at his obvious lie. "You are good at withholding information, wraith. But not creating falsehoods on a whim." I smirk and slip the stone into my pocket.

He snarls but says nothing more. Anger flickers in his eyes, but I only smile, happy to have something to use against him for the first time in our relationship. If he wants to tell me the truth about the jewel, then perhaps I'll reconsider. Until then, it's coming with me.

I walk back to the path, look out over the flat grey stones, and step out onto the first.

"Stop. Where are you going?"

"To find Rev."

"He abandoned you, and you continue to follow him?"

"Yes," I say, clearly and determined, as I skip over the stones, wondering what sick horrors are certain to find me in just moments.

30
REV

Pain rages through my body. Every muscle clenching. I wriggle, trying to gain even an inch of movement, but I can't. I'm trapped. And I know, without a doubt, that I am going to die.

It's cold here, beneath the shade of the largest tree I've ever seen. It towers over the whole valley. There is a short mountain, streaming smoke into the sky. Somewhere, here, lies the spell book. The book I need to save the fae realm and become the hero I was so determined to be.

The selfish, brash, stupid hero.

My redemption is right there, just a few feet away—and there's just one thing standing my way now.

The Night Terror.

Or, well, more specifically, her beast. My heart hammers in my chest as I stand face to face with the manticore. The roots of this massive tree have taken hold of me. It dragged me down below ground to some hidden cove where I can see nothing but blackness.

The tree's roots crush my chest and the ground

rumbles, dirt and stone crumbling beneath me. I cry out as the roots pull me down into the depths of the soil.

I can't breathe. Can't see. There is only pressure and pain and darkness.

Then, I'm in open stale air but my sight is still entirely blocked. I cough the dirt from my mouth and lungs. Part of me wonders if I shouldn't just stop trying and let it consume me.

Suffocation would certainly be a gentler death than whatever the manticore or the Night Terror have planned.

The rustling I've come to associate with wraith magic sounds before me. "Reahgan," I mutter.

His only response is nervous murmuring. I can't see him, but the air shifts with his movements. Though he seems agitated, he's not nearly as bothered that I am trapped in a tree from hell—literally—as he should be.

I don't have the breath to even ask him what he's doing or when he decided to turn on me. Perhaps it was when I fought him. When I flung him into the tar swamp and chose his murderer over him.

Even so, I didn't think he'd purposefully harm me.

He'd call me a fool and find a way to murder my fated mate and expect me to understand. But... set up a trap? Have me taken by the nightmarish beast from the valley of judgment?

The manticore chuckles, low and slow. His hot breath huffs into my face, smelling of rotten flesh. Likely his food supply if he has one. I choke on the smell, and my already stressed lungs beg for release, burning. My vision flickers, my mind spins. I can't... I....

My eyelids flutter.

This would be a kind death, I think.

The roots beneath me rumble with an amused chuckle. They clench tighter, causing a helpless cry to escape my lips, but just as I can feel the life seeping from my body, they loosen.

Breath rushes back into my lungs without my permission, and I gasp for breath.

"Such a fragile creature," an echoing voice rumbles from behind the tree. Beneath it? Inside it? I can't tell.

"No better than humans," the manticore agrees.

"Only a tad more *useful*." The voice drags out the words deliberately.

"Not this one, surely?" the manticore growls. I continue to suck in breaths like my life depends on it.

"Oh, this one most of all. Aside from our little blond pet, that is."

The manticore prowls around me, the pads of his massive paws gentle on the ash-like dirt of the underground cove. It must be a large cavern for him to walk freely, but it feels small. Filled with smells of soil and decay.

"He is no different from any other," he growls, displeased.

"True," the bodiless voice hums. "He is more powerful than some, less than many. He is easy to manipulate. A complete fool..."

"Thanks." I choke at her list of insults.

"There are many more, if you'd like?" the voice singsongs.

Something shifts in front of me, and I blink, trying to see anything. The Night Terror must be here, but where?

I jump as a sharp claw presses to the skin of my cheek, dragging down gently.

"No? All right then."

I swallow, and the tree behind me rumbles with laughter.

"This one's value comes because the child we require loves him."

The manticore growls.

"She will do anything to save her beloved mate, she's proved that time and time again. Regardless of the fact that he doesn't even feel the same. Pathetic."

"That's not true," I spit. Even knowing it's useless to converse with these creatures.

"Ahh, would you sacrifice yourself then? Would you allow her to depart from these lands and leave you behind?"

My stomach sinks. I... My breath catches. *Yes*, I decide. That quick. I would if I had to. But I always knew she wouldn't go. There was nothing I could do to force her through those gates without me. Not without...

"Ahh, yes. All you need, child... is to die."

My heart sinks. Did she just complete my thoughts?

"Would you do so willingly?" the voice purrs. "If it were to save her?"

A jolt of warning quivers through me. She's baiting me, I know. But between the fear and guilt and pain, it's so hard not to go there. Would I? And if I wouldn't... what does that say about me?

Selfish. Stupid. Pathetic.

"Caelynn, your mate who sacrificed her whole life to allow you to keep yours. She could live. She could earn the freedom she's always craved. You could give her that. All you have to do is... *cease to be.*"

A sharp pain shoots through my whole body from something sharp pressing between my vertebrae. I clench my jaw, and my mind spins out of control. I can't think. I can't...

"Hey," Reahgan cries through the darkness. "That was not part of the deal." But his quick passion flames out quickly.

"There were no deals, you stupid wraith. You are no better than them. An infant in our eyes. Naïve and short-sighted. Death is a mercy. You will come to understand that soon enough."

The pressure on my back eases, and I gasp for breath again. I have to think. I have to...

The pain hits me again. Only, this time, it's inside of me. Poison rushes through my veins, burning through every inch it touches, and very quickly, it's all of me.

"I will not kill you, child," the voice whispers. "Not yet."

31
CAELYNN

I skip over the smooth stones, muscles weighing heavier and heavier as I approach the center of these dark lands. *I'll be glad to breathe fresh air again...*

My heart sinks when I realize that I never will. My chest tightens, making it harder and harder to force in much-needed oxygen.

Black spots pepper my vision. But I move because that's what I must do. I'll help Rev one final time before letting him go forever.

Maybe I should be glad for those moments together, those little fragments of time we were able to carve out of an otherwise horrific experience, but my heart is so broken I can't... All I can think is that *he left.*

That it's over. I may never see him again.

I swallow and push those thoughts back again. I can't right now. Rev will soon face the Night Terror. My mate. *Live a good life for me,* I mentally ask of him. That's what I want.

That's all that's left to fight for—someone else's life. God, that's hard.

Sudden pressure on my lungs causes me to cough. I stop, one hand over my mouth and one on my stomach.

I'll never feel the sun on my skin. I never see a sincere smile.

I swallow through the lump in my throat and fight back a sob. Shit. Why now? Why did it have to hit me now?

Rev isn't here. He's gone. And I don't know for sure if he's okay. And I'm stuck in this place forever. My life is over.

And I'm so damn tired.

"Child?" my wraith whispers, his voice absent of his usual snarky tone.

I suck in a few desperate breaths and blink back tears. I'm okay. It's okay. I have a purpose, and when that's done, when the spell book is collected and Rev out of this cursed place, I can fall apart.

I will fall apart.

I won't survive him leaving. I realize that now. Because the darkness of this place, the curse, the death everywhere, it's slowly suffocating me.

"Caelynn," the wraith says more firmly. "Are you all right?"

"No, of course not." I rub my face rigorously and then stand up straight. "I'm fine. It's fine. Let's go."

I continue jumping over the murky water, feet balancing gently on each smooth footstone. Other than the smell, there isn't much significance about this place. There are faces beneath the surface here. Bodies of fallen fae, I'm guessing, stuck in a state of recent death. Perhaps there is more to it. Perhaps they're all me. I don't know. I don't allow myself to look closely enough.

I'm too busy trying not to throw up or pass out as the air grows thicker with fog. As ash rains from the sky.

"Slow down," the wraith barks.

I run faster, leaping over the stones.

"It is not a race, Caelynn," he yells like a father reprimanding a foolish child.

Yes, it is. It's a race to see if I'll fall apart before I make it to the edge of this swamp.

"If you fall in, you'll never come out. One touch of the water…"

"You're not helping!" I yell. My limbs are numb, my breath shaking.

"Stop if you must," he says more gently. "Collect yourself."

"I can't," I breathe. I pull at the shadows near me to fuel me. To comfort me like they have so many times. Instead, they suck me dry.

I scream as I realize, they are not my friend. Here in this place, even the shadows are against me. I force my magic to the front of my mind, and I dive through shadows full of teeth and resistance, and I leap. Why does the bank seem to be growing farther and farther?

I shadow leap again, screaming in agony as I do. Even my own magic is working against me now.

"Caelynn!" the wraith hollers. "If you miss even one step—"

I leap again, his voice cutting off.

"I cannot catch you!"

I leap again, farther now. I stop breathing. My vision is

rimmed with red. My head throbbing. I don't know if I'm going to make it.

Again. And again. One more, I tell myself.

One more, I say again.

ONE MORE—I throw everything I have into it because if I don't make it to the bank I will fall here and now, and I will never rise from those waters. I don't know what's in them. I don't care. Even if they were pure spring water, I'd be done for.

I fall to my knees the moment I hit soggy ground, fingers digging into the dirt. It's... warm. Tears fall freely now, splashing over my fingers, which I realize are coated in red.

My hand is slick with bright red blood. My stomach heaves and this time, it's not a false alarm.

I haven't eaten in over a day, but the small contents of my stomach unfurl themselves onto the blood-soaked ground. A dismembered finger lies just feet ahead. Mangled flesh lines the whole bank, and I almost pass out.

"Move, Caelynn," the wraith orders. "Over there. I'd carry you if I could, but..."

My limbs don't have the ability to carry me now. But I look to where he's pointing. At the bottom of a mountain, there is a short stretch of open ground where it seems the seeping wound ends. I swallow.

Block it out, Cae. If there is one thing you've always been good at, it's blocking out the worst bits. Focus and move.

I close my eyes and push through my pain. I keep my eyes closed, and I crawl over the mushy ground. My whole body trembles. I picture a simple swamp of dirt and algae. That's all this is, I tell myself.

My nose tells a different story. I cannot block out the smell of putrid flesh. I stop and wretch a second time, still not daring to open my eyes.

"Keep going," the wraith whispers. "You're doing good. Keep moving. I'll tell you when you can rest."

Rest, I think. It sounds like such a lovely word. But I don't even know what that feels like. My bottom lip trembles and tears begin their stream down my cheeks again.

Why was this so hard? Why now?

Because he abandoned you, a voice whispers.

No, I think.

He thinks you're dead. And he doesn't care. The darkness presses in on me. It bites at my soul, carving away pieces of it. Bit by bit. My own shadows that once comforted me. That once held me like a parent when I had none.

My heart roars with the pain of a final heartbreak—of betrayal.

This is how I will die. This is what my life has come to.

"Keep going, Caelynn. You are strong. So much stronger than they think." He's shouting now. Can he see how close I am to giving up? "Prove it to them!"

But what if they're right? I don't even have the energy to say the words aloud.

"A few more feet," he coaches.

I force my muscles on.

I can do this, I think. I won't stop until I can't anymore.

"One more," he whispers.

My hand reaches a powdery substance, and I push again until my knees are on dry ground. My body collapses there in a fit of sobs.

"Shh," my wraith coos over my fallen body.

My breaths are quick and shallow, my mind spinning. I curl my fingers into the dry dirt. It sticks and clots over my blood-soaked hands, but I don't care. I cling to it.

Smokey and thick, the air is no more comforting than before. It hurts to breathe in, burning my lungs, but I gulp it in anyway.

"You made it, dear," he tells me. "You're very strong, my girl."

"Doesn't feel like it," I whisper.

"Trust me. You are."

32
REV

Slowly, my mind clears from the haze set over it. I can't see anything more than before—pitch black. I taste bitter smoke in every pained breath.

The poison stings inside my veins, tingling uncomfortably, but the burn has settled into a dull ache. Every muscle weighs a hundred pounds, but my mind is clearing, heart picking up speed as I remember what's happened.

Caelynn didn't make it through the fire wall. She's gone.

My heart cracks all over again. It's what she wanted. To die here. But I wanted to prove her wrong so badly. I wanted to give something, anything, back to her.

She'd lost so much.

I failed.

Then, I was taken by the manticore, so I've failed myself too.

I push against my heavy restraints but find they have not changed. Wood curls against my chest and arms, gripping them like strong arms, sharp branches digging in like fingers.

I blink rapidly, trying to adjust to the darkness, but I can't make out anything.

Is the manticore nearby? I don't hear him now. I only feel the dark presence of something... ancient. Powerful.

I shiver. The Night Terror is here.

"He wakes." The branches holding me tremble along with the deep voice.

I cough. "What do you want?"

Something shifts before me. A being massive but smooth. Power sizzles through the darkness. The Night Terror doesn't respond.

Why hold me like this? "Don't you want to kill me and be done with it?"

"Killing you did seem convenient once upon a time, yes. But unfortunately for you, my little pet, I've found a better purpose for you."

A blade presses to my back, carving through my leather clothing and splitting the skin. I groan and squirm to no avail. The blade halts at a shallow cut.

A shape moves through the darkness, and my breath shudders. What *is* she?

"Pain is enjoyable. But it is not all I desire from your extended life. Would you like to see what I see, my pet?"

I curl my lip.

"Your mate has made it through the swamp."

Caelynn is alive? My heart bursts with hope only to crash back down. I am here, and it's only a matter of time before they get their hands on her too. She told me herself the moment she learned they had me, she'd come running.

The tree vibrates beneath me, purring like a pleased kitten.

We were supposed to fight together. We could have—

"Did you really think you had a chance against me, foolish child? No better than a hopeful puppy. Even together, you could not defeat me. You cannot win this battle." The voice shifts and cool puffs of air hit my cheek.

I let out a pained breath, lungs burning. Caelynn isn't dead yet, but maybe she was right all along. To win this game, she has to die. Loss washes over me again. I was just stupid to think there was hope to save her. Stubborn and foolish.

"Foolish, indeed." The powerful voice sends waves of terror through me. "To think that victory would be so easy. Your mate's death would be only the beginning, my pet."

The massive slumping form shifts to the other side. "How loyal are you, dog?" She breathes on my neck. "That is what I wonder. You vowed to protect the world. Would you choose your mate over your duty? Or will you allow her to face her worst nightmares to save you over and over again? What will you do, dog, when I carve into her body like a knife through butter?"

Agony wracks through my body, muscles clenching at the thought of her pain.

"Will you endure her screams to retain your honor? Or will you do exactly as I ask to save her?"

"Where is she," I grumble, pulling at the tight restraints over my arms and chest.

"Would you like to see? It's quite a sad sight, I'll warn you. But oh, I suppose I could oblige for a moment or two."

My vision flashes, a landscape appearing before me. The swamp. I'm far over the water glistening softly.

Shadows puff in and out, traveling farther and farther over the waters. Once, twice, a third time.

Is she shadow walking?

"I have always admired that ability. Of course, the only reason she has it is because my mate gave it to her. She is only strong because of him. And soon, her strength will be ours."

Caelynn falls to the bank on her hands and knees, and blood splatters. My stomach sinks. I don't even know if the vision is real, but my soul cries out to her. *Be okay, Caelynn. Please.*

"Don't you see it, my pet?"

I jump as sharp claws run down my cheek. My vision is still entirely on the swamp, seeing something not even here. I can't even be sure it's real...

"Your mate is dying. Would you like to watch as she wastes away? It's so achingly slow," the creature draws, her finger carving down my chest, a caress that splits the skin. I can feel the warm blood pooling on my skin, dripping slowly, though all I see is Caelynn.

The image shifts, circling as Caelynn crawls through several hundred feet of dismembered limbs.

"That's my handy work, you know?" the Night Terror brags. "There are so many of them—bodies unaltered—at the bottom of that swamp. The perfect medium for my art."

There is no pattern or beauty to the placement of the body parts. She just enjoyed carving them up. I'd believe science over art.

Caelynn crawls desperately, her body moments from giving out. She gags into the piles of bodies. *Get up*, I think. *Keep fighting.*

There is a wraith hovering over her. My hands clench into fists. Is he helping her or hurting her? I can't tell if he cares for her at all, or if he only wants something from her like she suggests.

Caelynn continues pushing forward then finally, falls onto her face in the mud just past the pile of body parts.

"She is giving up," the beast whispers delicately, and a sob builds in my chest.

"If she dies," I whisper, voice hoarse, heartbroken—but angry. Vindictive. "You lose."

A roar of laughter sends shockwaves over my body. The tree beneath me vibrates with pleasure. "If only you knew how wrong you are, my pet."

"What do you mean?" I breathe. I'm sure I shouldn't be conversing with this thing no matter what. The vision might not even be true. Her words very well could be complete fabrications, but I can't help it. My wounded soul is thirsty for understanding.

"Caelynn's death would result in her losing her ability to reverse my curse. This is true. But," the branches clench around me, squeezing me so tightly I can't breathe, "there is a difference between the death of the body and death of the soul."

The branches loosen their grip, and air rushes back through my lungs.

"If she gives up and allows herself to die, her soul would die first. And it'd be all too easy for my mate to keep her body alive just long enough for his magic to revive her.

There are two ways we can achieve our goals. One is convincing Caelynn to do our bidding. That is where you come in, child. She is in love with you. Pathetic as you may be. She has proved time and time again that she will give anything for you. But that is only my backup plan. I have an easier scheme in mind."

The Night Terror slithers around me, her voice echoing. She still shows me the vision of Caelynn lying in the mud with the wraith wafting over her.

"We will break her," the Night Terror whispers in my ear. "And indeed, we are so very close already."

No.

"We will dismantle her soul piece by piece until she gives up entirely. Her soul is so very dim already. When it dies, and it will, she will lose the ability to control his magic. He will regain its control, and then he would have everything he'd ever need."

My blood runs cold. "Because his magic is inside of her." *Shit.*

I see it now. Why they backed off. Why the wraiths spied but never confronted. Why even the manticore looked us in the eye but then turned around, leaving us with no more than a few disturbing words.

They were waiting for Caelynn to give up. To let herself die.

That's what's been happening to her. That's why she's been so exhausted, her magic so volatile. I was right—I was losing her. And the wolf was right—the Night Bringer's magic is the key to their success. They're suffocating her from the inside out.

"Yes," she whispers. "He can only use it if she destroys

herself first. She is so very close to that fate. Now, we will simply enjoy the show…"

"No," I whisper. My despair explodes from my chest, rushing from my dark prison, seeking my mate. *Find her. Keep her safe.* I beg, knowing it's more than futile.

Rage swells in my chest, burning so hot I can hardly contain it. White-hot flame burst forth from my chest, completely outside of my control, and my tree prison parts, writhing in pain. Its hiss echoes through my mind, but I stumble forward.

A small whisper of white light flashes from my chest, shooting away into the darkness.

———

My boots sink into the muck as I run, feet pumping over the ashen ground, slick with the blood of long-dead, unknown fae.

She's only feet ahead, blond hair spread wide, face pale as snow. I fall to my knees beside her and grip her shoulders tightly.

"Ow," she mumbles, face crumpled in pain. "Rev?"

A desperate cry of relief escapes me, and without thinking, I crash my lips onto hers, just needing to feel her, be near her.

My magic follows, hurtling through her, frantic to find the cause of her ailment. To help her. Fix her. Heal her.

Her back arches and she groans against my lips, a much more pleasant sound than the last.

"Rev," she says again.

I pull back, lips and magic alike, and peer into her pitch-black eyes.

"What happened?" I ask.

"What happened to you? He said you left... you..."

"I... the manticore took me. I was trapped."

Her face crumbles. Agony covers every feature.

"I'm okay now," I whisper. "I'm here." My fingers drift over her cheek.

The wraith hisses. "You were trapped by her? Then how are you here now?"

I narrow my eyes at the wraith.

"She wouldn't let you go once in her grasp." He turns and begins to pace back and forth, barely hovering over the ground. "It doesn't make sense," he mutters.

"I used my magic against my restraints and..."

"Foolish child. Your magic is strong against wraiths, but it would do no better than any other against hers. She only released you if she wanted you released."

I blink rapidly as my vision blinks to solid black darkness and then back. The pressure of tree limbs crushes my chest against its trunk. It's hard to breathe.

"Caelynn." I turn my attention back to the beautiful fae in my arms, the fae so very close to losing her life and her soul. I would blame myself if she did. I didn't do enough. There must have been more I could have done to give her hope, to give her life.

If she gives up now, he'll take over. He'll win.

"Caelynn," I whisper, tears in my eyes. I lean in and press my lips gently to hers just before the Night Terror rips me back into her talons.

33
CAELYNN

Ash falls from the sky, drifting gently toward my arms blotched with dirt and blood. My eyelids flutter as I watch it land on my forearm and stick.

"Rev?" I groan, rolling onto my stomach awkwardly and pulling myself onto my hands and knees.

"Rev left you, remember?" My wraith's voice is quiet, but there is a bite to his words. He doesn't like me talking about Rev.

"No. He was here. He was just here..."

The wraith sighs. "Child, you are seeing things."

I press my eyes closed. "No," I whisper. I still feel it. His magic filled me for a moment. He was trying to heal me from my imaginary wounds. He can't heal me from what's destroying me from the inside. The magic, the curse, is sucking me dry. Or maybe it's the hopelessness of my situation. Maybe Rev was right. Maybe I have given up.

"He's not here?"

"No, child," my wraith says.

"Why are you helping me?" I ask, lying back down on the ashy ground. Behind me only a few hundred feet, the slope of the mount begins. There, somewhere, the spell book is hidden. So close.

That also means Rev must be nearby. He'll have begun the trek up the mountain.

If I can make myself stand up and walk, maybe I can find him. Maybe I can find them both. Maybe I can have one last moment with him before I die. Before I let this place devour me.

"Don't you know this already?"

"Not really," I admit, staring up blankly at the hazy sky. Smoke plumes from the mount behind me. A volcano more than a mountain. *That makes it so much better.*

"You're my hope," my wraith whispers.

"For the Shadow Court? In death, that is still what matters most to you?"

"You are my redemption. If I can rebuild the court I helped to dismantle..." He pauses, gliding around my fallen body in a tight circle. "But also, I've come to realize that you are here because of me, child. I don't know if you realize that. It's my fault. It's my blood in your veins that marked you as a target for these horrific beasts." The pain in his voice is sharp. His smoke-like magic is continually restless, but he mimics me, lying down and staring up at the grey sky. There are no clouds to examine here. No changing skies. No birds in flight. There is only a sheet of smog, never changing other than to dim and brighten over a day's time.

Still, the wraith lies beside me on the ashen ground, his magic rippling awkwardly as he does.

"There have been many with that same blood since your death."

He nods. "There was a small manner of luck involved, yes."

I shake my head. "No. They chose me for a reason. They saw the darkness inside. They saw my reckless ambition and used it against me."

"You are a foolish child sometimes." He tsks. "Ambition is not unique to you. And recklessness is simply a common adolescent trait. The things they took advantage of do not make you bad. You never desired to cause pain. I can see that in your eyes. In your soul. In your every action. You have fought for good. You have given all of yourself, much more than another fae would have given, to help those you care for. I admire you for this, Caelynn. If I'm honest, I think the Night Bringer failed by choosing *you* as his tool. So many others would have been easier to manipulate. To trick. He underestimated you. And you are close, very close, to winning his game."

"I'm also very close to losing it."

"Yes," he whispers. "Yes, you are close to that too."

"It's not over, though, is it? Even if I were to walk out of here alive... he'd come for me again."

"He couldn't," the wraith breathes. "You ensured that with your bargain so long ago. You don't fully understand how well you did that day, or perhaps, how badly he did. To those who know what you've done, you are a true hero. The Night Bringer tried to trick you. He wanted you as his eternal slave. It was the simplest way to achieve his ends. But he knew no bargain could convince you to willingly submit to slavery. And so, he presented a false bargain. It had to be real, of course, or else the result would be false. Magic cannot be fooled. Instead, he created a bargain he knew you would fail. He wanted you to kill the wrong fae, and when you did, he would use it against you. The bargain would have trapped you. That is why he gave you as beneficial of terms as he did. He never expected you to figure it out."

My wraith sighs. "Refuse, maybe. Fail, possibly. Succeed in what you assumed was the right murder but was not, yes. Any of those results earned him exactly what he desired. But to kill Reahgan? To fulfill the true bargain? No. He did not think it possible you'd figure it out and succeed."

"But I did," I croak.

"And because of that, the Night Bringer cannot touch you now. You are in full control of his magic, and that gives you an advantage. His only way to manipulate you now is with your mate. The mate you saved. The mate you sacrificed so deeply for. He was right, that you'd throw anything away to save him. If you were to leave the Schorchedlands now, you could take back your throne and the Night Bringer couldn't touch you because that was part of his bargain."

I close my eyes and hold my breath. "But the scourge would continue to spread."

"You could find another way to stop that silly plague."

"Could we?"

"Certainly," he says, voice high pitched.

But I am certain he doesn't believe it. Maybe we could. Maybe we couldn't. "And if I were to have children?"

The wraith is silent, his magic continues to billow and

ripple, but he does not speak. My children, and their children, will not be safe so long as the Night Bringer and Night Terror are living. That much is clear. I would have to choose to never have children or raise them in a different court where they would absorb a different elemental magic to free them of my curse.

"Why do they want Rev dead?" This is a question I hadn't bothered to ask previously. Something about his magic, his fate, I don't know. I should have asked. I should have clarified.

"He has the power to undo their curse. He has the power to heal what no one else can heal."

I purse my lips. "Like the Scourge."

That's what this was always about, right? The plague. It feels almost small now in comparison to what I know the world will face if the Night Terror is freed.

"Indeed, Rev can put a stop to the scourge without the spell book."

"And yet, you still want him dead."

"I want you alive. He is of no consequence. In fact, if his survival didn't cost yours, I'd prefer him alive. Contrary to what you think, I do not wish you unhappiness. But that is not the reality we have now."

"And you hate me for choosing him over my homelands."

"I do not hate you. I am disappointed. I was certainly angry. But I do understand how it is an unfair choice."

My eyelids flutter closed. My mind is more at ease now, my heart rate has settled, but my body is still worn and tired. I feel… numb. I feel nothing.

"How are you, child?"

"I don't know," I whisper. I force my body upright and look down at my hands. I watch the ash fall and land on my skin. We are so very close to the center, where rumors told us a living being couldn't survive for more than a few hours. Does that mean the air is already poisoning me? Shouldn't the ash be burning?

I look down at my arm again. There are red dots where the flakes have struck. My skin is peeling off, grey like ash. I pick at it gently and a thick slice pulls pack, exposing red flesh. I gasp and drop it back.

What is happening to me? This acid rain is burning, but I don't feel it. I don't feel anything anymore.

And how did I know the ash would burn? Did I read that somewhere? I don't remember reading or hearing about it.

But I do remember dreaming about it.

I remember a dream that I was running through the center of the Schorchedlands to reach Rev, to save him. He was in trouble.

I remember my wraith being with me, telling me to let him die. Telling me that the Night Bringer would take over my soul if I wasn't careful.

"Where is Rev?" I ask again.

Was it really a dream, him healing me here? He... I swallow. He said he'd been trapped by the Night Terror. I whip my head to the wraith.

"Where is Rev," I demand this time, heart hammering in my chest. Something is wrong. I know it deep in my soul.

"How should I know?"

"You do," I say, eyes harsh. He's supported me, helped

me, but all I can feel is anger. Because he knows. He knows where Rev is. I reach to grip the wraith by the throat, but my hand falls right through his black smokey magic.

"What are you doing?"

Something is wrong... that dream. I had a dream. I was running to Rev. He was in trouble. And the wraith was telling me to leave him behind.

"If you stay," the wraith whispered, "the Night Bringer will take away more of you, piece by piece until it's only his magic that remains. Then, he will free himself with ease. It will be his soul inside your body, reigning over the Shadow Court. On that day, Caelynn, Princess of the Shadow Court, you'll lose every-thing you ever dared to hope for."

That's what the wraith wants.

Fuck.

"You're working with him," I whisper.

"What are you on about, child?"

My hand can't touch him. But my iron blade can. I grip the blade and have it pressed against his heart before he can even blink. "What did you do?"

The wraith freezes. Fear flickers over his expression, but then his lips spread into an eerie grin and he rumbles with a low chuckle. "You're going to kill me, are you?"

"Why is that funny?"

"I am your last ally, child. How ironic it would be for you to end me, leaving you entirely alone."

"Allies don't betray you. What did you do to Rev? I know you did something." I press harder over his magic which sizzles against the iron.

He winces but continues his sick grin. "Have you become as weak as we? Have you become like us?" the wraith whispers. "Perhaps you are less special than I thought. You're just like the rest of them."

"No, I'm the only one foolish enough to trust a wraith!"

"Then, end me. Kill me now. Relieve me of the despair I will feel when I watch you die and all my hopes end."

"I've always known I can't win this battle," I admit. "But I can stop them from winning. If I die, the line has ended."

"Your father still lives," the wraith whispers like a threat.

I drop the knife. I hadn't thought of that. Would he go after my father? "Is that even possible?"

"Probably not. But he'll try. He'll torture him. Perhaps try to force him to breed."

My fingers tremble.

"I swear, child. I am not lying when I say I am on your side. I do not wish for the Night Terror released from her prison or the Night Bringer to gain any additional power. I fought to stop them long ago. I have not turned back on that."

I lean closer, examining him. "You know what happened to Rev," I say more calmly. I believe him, I decide. He may not have jumped sides wholly, but he is certainly withholding information. "Be on my side entirely, and I will do my best to find a way out of this place and revive the Shadow Court."

His eyes narrow. "You'll promise that if you exit this place, you'll take your place as queen?"

I pull in a long breath, considering such a promise. I don't like making bargains of any kind. But a promise is not a binding bargain... and I would entirely intend to give my power to the Shadow Court and work to rebuild its power. If I can get out of that banishment...

I pull my blade from his chest. "I will do everything within my power to claim my throne," I promise. Then, I point at him. "And you will tell me *everything* you know about Rev. You will not purposefully withhold important information from us. And you will do everything you can to protect both Rev and me."

He curls his lips, exposing sharp teeth. "I cannot promise to protect him."

"You will."

"I will not." He spins and begins to pace. "I will promise instead to never cause him harm, directly or indirectly. I will not conspire to cause him harm or take action I know will harm him—unless it is to save you."

I screw my lips, thinking it through. "Rev told me he doesn't intend to leave me here," I admit, cheeks burning. I don't even understand such a proclamation. How could he not intend to leave me behind? What could he possibly do? "He is my ally. If you are to be mine, you will be his too."

The wraith sighs. "I will help him if I can, and if it doesn't hurt you in the process."

I grunt. I suppose it's good enough. "Very well. I agree."

The wraith's smile grows, his eyes flickering gold.

I look out over the open plain, to the mountain pass a few hundred feet away. Nothing but ash and stones between us. The swamp lies behind us, with its bank full of torn limbs and still warm flesh. About a mile to the east is a massive tree, grey bark, and sprawling leafless branches reaching up into the sky, nearly as tall as the volcano itself.

We're smack in the middle of these open lands, which

means we're sitting ducks. I haven't bothered to use my shadows in hours now. I haven't had the energy or the thought to do it. I haven't seen evidence of a single being other than the wraith.

"We need to move on and find Rev."

"About that—"

My eyes flash to him angrily.

He raises his hands in surrender. "Allies now, remember? I'll tell you everything, I promise."

"Where is he?"

The wraith pauses, eyes darting around nervously. "She has him."

My stomach drops to my feet. Part of me knew it, but even so, panic takes control for those terrible moments.

That dream or vision... his magic still tingles inside of me. He'd given me a jolt of power, of hope, I desperately needed.

But God, the thought of him in her grip, the pain she'll inflict, the terror—my hands shake.

"Is he alive?" I'm barely able to form the words. I know the answer to this too, and I'm not sure it's better than the alternative.

"Oh yes. She still intends to use him."

The Night Terror is going to use Rev the way the Night Bringer used me.

My vision flickers to black, and I feel myself falling.

My mind and soul are burning, but it's not like fire. It's like... acid.

I groan and roll, writhing in pain.

"Ahh, there she is," a deep echoing voice calls to me. "My little pet."

"Caelynn?" my wraith asks, and I shake my head, pushing the memories away. "What is happening? Tell me."

"Memories," I whisper.

"Of?"

"Him. The Night Bringer."

"He is trying to pull you under," the wraith whispers. "You must fight it, Caelynn."

I clench my jaw. The echo of pain long past slams into me and my vision flickers away, turning black for a second time.

Fire sears my back, and I writhe in pain. "Make," I force from my cracked lips. "It." I curl my hands into fits, pain putting pressure on every part of me. My mind. My body. My soul.

The ache is deeper than I even knew it went.

"Stop," I whine pathetically.

The Night Bringer chuckles. "Gladly," he rumbles in my ear. "Just agree to my bargain."

I groan, but the pain won't let up. "No," I finally get out.

He laughs again. "You think yourself very noble, don't you? But you forget, my little pet, I can see inside your head. I can see what you crave. What you would do to gain it. You and I... we are the saaaame."

———

My mind is released from the darkness, and I gasp like I'm breaking through the surface after nearly drowning.

"Are you all right?" my wraith asks.

I shake my head, panting in breath. "I don't know."

"Tell me what he showed you," the wraith says.

I bite my lip. "It was just a memory of when he trapped me. Before the bargain."

Is that what's happening to Rev now? Is he being tortured like I had been?

My mind spins. Is there even a way to win this now?

She will flay him alive.

I shake my head. It's so much. Too much. I don't know how to do this... I don't know what it all means. "Do you know if a soul can die while the body still lives?"

My wraith blinks. "Yes."

"How?"

"Often, that happens with suicide. The body simply dies moments after. Depression can suck the life from the soul, like an illness on your mind instead of your body. That is usually what it means. The body cannot live without a soul, though. And so, it doesn't make much difference. Soul, mind, body—if one shatters completely, the rest follow."

"The body cannot live without a soul... Except mine has two," I whisper. The Night Bringer gave me more than just a bit of magic, I realize.

I curse under my breath.

"How could you have two?" my wraith asks sincerely.

"He went straight up Harry Potter," I spit and slap the ground. The blood has dried, and it's starting to flake.

"You've lost me, child."

"His magic. It will live on if my soul dies. He will take over my body."

I've been so very close to giving up, so close to letting that happen. Close to thinking I have nothing to live for. I do. I have to slap these creatures in their face one more time. I have to take back my mate. Again. I have to never let them take me like that.

"The Night Terror wants me to come for Rev," I say.

"Yes," my wraith hisses. "It's what she expects. That is why..."

Why he didn't tell me. I wave him off. I don't know if he was right or wrong. It doesn't matter. Not now.

It's certainly my first thought. I have to get to him. But... how? Do I march into her lair and challenge her to a battle? Even in a battle of wits, I'd have no chance of winning in my current state.

No, I have only one move if I refuse to give up. It may mean playing right into her hands, but I know I have access to the one thing the Night Terror needs. If I don't get it, she'll only continue to emotionally torture me until my soul dies and the Night Bringer takes over my body. Lose-lose. I need to grab the cards while they're in my reach.

34
REV

The Night Terror is angry when she realizes what I did. I can feel it in the tightness of the tree branches clenching my arms and chest. In the steady vibration of her pet. How the purr of my tree-prison changes into a growl.

Then, out of the darkness, something shifts, slithering closer. "What," her low voice sends terror through my body—I can't help it, "did you do?"

The very ground trembles with her voice. The vines trapping me clench even tighter and a groan escapes my lips.

I try to ignore the panic rushing through my veins and remember I'd do it again. I'd do anything to help Caelynn.

"You'd do anything to save her. Or you'd do anything to *help her* save *you*?"

My teeth chatter, breath caught in my lungs.

"You'll pay for your insubordination." A sharp blade presses to the soft spot under my chin.

"Every pet must be trained," a deep voice sounds through the darkness. Not the Night Terror.

The ground rumbles with laughter, the blade pressing to my neck bounces, pressure easing, and growing. I wince at the sting.

"Very true. How should I punish his bad behavior?"

Several booms ricochet through the space. Footsteps? Is it the manticore?

"Pain," the voice answers with a hiss of pleasure.

"Are you offering aid in this endeavor? Are you experienced in training willful beings?"

"Experienced? Perhaps not. A willing learner? Most definitely."

"Very well, my beast, as a reward for your obedience, you may punish the fae prince. But he must not die. If he dies, you will follow him quickly."

The blade recedes from my neck, and she slithers away. "Have fun with your toy." Her laughter resounds through the darkness, but then the branches holding me loosen their grip and I fall to the ground. I expected dirt or mud but instead find solid stone.

My heart pounds, muscles already tense, waiting for the pain to come.

Another three booming footsteps, and then I can feel his breath on my face. The manticore picks me up by my leg, hanging me in the air like a rag doll. I hold back any cries or whimpers of fear. I won't give him the satisfaction —not yet at least.

I don't expect I'll be able to help myself soon.

"Ready to begin, child?"

35
CAELYNN

Every step of the way, I've followed their plan.

The Night Bringer wanted me to follow Rev into the Schorchedlands. That's why Rev's father exposed his deal with the Night Bringer only after I'd broken Rev's heart and he'd fled toward the Wicked Gates.

It was part of their plan.

The Night Bringer wanted me to let Reahgan kill me. He wanted me to give up and allow my own death.

He left us be for a while because he wanted us to remain in these cursed lands longer to weaken my body and to give these cursed lands longer to erode my soul.

Now, his mate has taken my mate. He expects me to come for him.

I pull myself to my feet, feeling Rev's comforting magic tingling in my veins, and stare out at the two paths before me.

"Where is he?" I whisper.

My wraith floats beside me, looking out at the final square mile of the Schorchedlands. Slowly, he lifts his cloaked arm and clawed finger to point toward a massive tree to the east of the mountain. The tree is grey with streaks of white and thousands of branches curling out like claws reaching to the sky.

"And the spell book?" I know very little about its specific location.

He shakes his head but points to the mountain that covers half the red sky. No new information there.

Over the peak is a steady stream of thick black smoke. I don't know the exact altitude, but by sight, I'd guess it would take me two hours to climb it, and that's using as much of my strength and magic as possible and going straight up, not searching along every end.

"What do I need to know about the mountain?"

The wraith stills, but I keep my eyes trained on the last massive obstacle before me.

"This is my first time on this side of the wall," he admits. "I've never been there. I've only heard stories."

Never? He only crossed the fire wall because of us, then. "Were you afraid of the fire?"

"I am afraid of judgment, yes. We all are; otherwise, we wouldn't be wraiths."

"So, it wasn't just me then." I smirk. He grunts.

I'm tempted to ask him about his trip over the flames. There is very little I know about him. Did the spirit of the Wicked Gates speak to him too? But I wouldn't want to get into my own experience, so I assume he wouldn't either.

My spirit is failing. Crossing the swamp while believing Rev had left without me just minutes after learning I'd apparently died was enough to nearly derail me.

I pull in a long breath, recentering my motivation.

Death will come but not yet.

Right now, I have an ancient, powerful being to piss off and a mate to save.

"Since we're officially allies now, I should probably stop calling you wraith. What is your name?"

"Call me Darren."

"Darren Shadowspell," I murmur. I suppose history should have told me that one.

I read about him and his family as a child. Over and over. I adored history. But there was so much truth missing from those pages. Perhaps if I make it out of here, I'll write the full story. Even if no one will believe me, putting it down on paper would make it feel more real. More complete.

You will never have the chance. My breath catches.

Well, perhaps I'll ask Rev to do it for me. One final request.

Remember me. Remember my ancestors. Remember the sacrifice my people made to save us all from those beasts.

But then again, I never told Rev about my full heritage. He doesn't know who Darren is. He doesn't know I am the rightful heir to the Shadow Court throne. That piece of the puzzle may always be missing.

Or maybe, as he research for the project, he'll uncover the truth. Maybe my parents will talk with him. Maybe they'll tell him.

I swallow. I haven't seen my mother and father since I was seventeen. Ten years ago. I take in a long breath.

Don't give up. Not yet.

Seek the right death.

I will die. That's what the Wicked Gates told me, right? I just have to die at the right time, in the right way.

"Tell me what you know about the mountain as we travel. It may take a while for us to climb it."

My wraith—Darren—pauses, his eyes widening. Then, he nods. And we begin the journey the Night Terror won't expect.

We're going to get the book first and pray to God, Rev will still be alive once I've obtained my needed leverage.

36
REV

All I know is pain. My vision flickers between red and black.

Bones shatter. Blood splatters.

"You're going to kill him," a rough voice says. I don't know who. I don't care who it could possibly be. It doesn't matter.

The creature standing over me growls and drops me into a heap on the stone ground. "Would you like to take his place?"

"I'd like him to live. And so would your master."

Another growl sends a tremor through my body.

"His body will fail quickly."

"I've hardly begun!" my torturer complains. "He cannot be that weak."

"You've done a great job of... punishing him. If you stop now, you'll likely get the chance to hurt him again. If you continue, you'll break his mind or body. Your master may appreciate a broken mind, but you'll never be able to punish him again. If you break his body, she'll break yours."

The stranger must win the argument because the ground trembles beneath me with booms growing more and more distant.

"Rev," a voice whispers.

I try to force my eyes open to no avail. I try to speak, but I can't open my lips.

"It's me," the voice claims. "Reahgan."

The mention of my brother's name shocks my mind back into focus. Reahgan. My brother. He came to my rescue.

"You'll be okay," Reahgan claims. I've never felt pain like this. It didn't last long, I don't think. The manticore slammed me against the stone a few times, and after that, I can't remember much.

"Can you heal yourself? That will help."

I groan. I don't want to move even an inch. My magic squirms beneath my skin, but I don't have the energy to command it. "Caelynn," I mutter.

I can hear the annoyance in Reahgan's voice as he speaks his next words. "She's fine, so far. I don't know why you care. She left you to be tortured to death."

I blink rapidly. I have a hard time telling if my sight returns to normal because wherever we are is pitch black. Eventually, I'm able to command a bit more of my body. I can move my legs and arms, though the pain is intense.

My stomach churns as I attempt to move.

"Stay still, you fool," Reahgan tells me. "Heal your brain first then your bones. You're certain to have a major concussion and possibly internal bleeding. That beast is lucky you've got healing abilities, or you may have died anyway."

I groan, trying to push my dizzy mind into submission. Finally, my magic sparks and warms inside my mind. Reahgan is right, my brain is swelling. Panting, I push the magic to stitch my brain tissue back together. My limbs roar in pain, my vision spinning. But after a few minutes, my mind has returned to, well, close to normal.

It's still hard to think with so much of my body in excruciating pain. I can't move without agitating shattered bones. It may take a long while to heal the rest of it. And damn, I don't want to use all of my magic. But what else can I do?

"You might," I say between tense breaths, "want to tell your master that if he does that again, I won't have the magic left to heal myself."

"My master?"

I grunt. "She is, isn't she?"

"No. I made one bargain with her to save your life. That's all."

"Mhmm." I don't know Reahgan's full intentions, but I don't believe he's truly on my side. "Caelynn?" I ask again. I need to know she's okay.

"She'll never love you."

I groan. "I didn't ask you about our relationship."

"You didn't ask me anything. You muttered the whore's name."

A ragged growl escapes my lips, anger simmering, but I don't have the energy for any more than that. "Don't you dare…" I seethe.

"All right, all right. She's a saint. She only murdered me in cold blood."

"After you captured her. And threatened her. Hurt her."

"Semantics."

"Facts."

"She still ended my life. Aren't I allowed to be bitter?"

"Be bitter. Don't call her names."

He grunts in annoyance, and I take the moment to drag more magic to my limbs. I have several broken ribs, and my femur is snapped, but I first heal my shattered shoulder.

"Your mate is living. She is not under the control of the Night Terror. Yet."

She'll never love you. Dammit. I hate that those words get under my skin. "Why do you think she'll never love me?"

Reahgan chuckles. "Couldn't resist, could you? She loves you in some kind of way, clearly, or she wouldn't have been willing to sacrifice all she has for you. But she can't ever love you the way you want. The way a mate should love the other."

I swallow. "Why?"

"Because she is broken."

"No," I say, but my heart aches, and part of me wonders if he is right. She is broken, her heart has been broken for a full decade. But that can heal...

"She can't ever accept love from you because she hasn't forgiven herself."

My heart sinks, realizing it's true. She's never felt hope for herself. She's been so ready to die. Not because she doesn't want to live, but because she thinks it's what she deserves.

37
CAELYNN

My feet pound on the ashen ground, sprinting over the rubble.

Dark fluid flutters from the sky like flurries of snow, except instead of the gentle sting of frost, it's the harsh bite of acid. The searing pain scatters over every inch of exposed skin, leaving red welts behind, but I clench my jaw and push through the discomfort.

The air is thick and hot, the poison in the atmosphere getting stronger. Will I even know it when I reach the place where a mortal cannot survive even an hour? Or was that an exaggeration? It hurts, but I've already been here for an hour.

Am I dying without even knowing it?

Will the Night Bringer even allow me to die this way? He needs me. She needs me.

I don't know the answers to any of those questions—I only know what I must do.

Every lungful sends more pain cascading through my chest, but I don't dare focus on that now.

Do you remember what it felt like?

I stumble but catch myself and continue running up the slope.

When I carved through your body? When I tortured you and ripped away your soul?

No! I roar in my own mind. *You never took my soul.*

Sick laughter—not my own—rumbles within my chest. *No, I just gave you mine.*

I hold back a whimper, tears stinging my eyes. "You can't have me," I whisper through quick breaths.

"What?" Darren demands.

"Nothing!" I yell.

He did tell me that the mountain will give us visions. There will be spirits here more powerful than even wraiths. The ancient and powerful beings that once ruled the earth but have lost their dominion. Those the Night Bringer and Terror have defeated in their time.

They are trapped, their power contained under the rock making up this mountain. The closer we get, the more we'll feel their power—even be influenced by it.

I push all of it from my mind. I can't focus on what I'm leaving behind, on what may be happening to Rev.

I run faster, barely able to hold my magic in check. Yes, I could move quicker if I shadow walk, but my magic is already low and I'll need every ounce I can cling to.

That's all there is now, all I can allow—pain and determination. I run because I must. I try to use the pain to my advantage; I try to become the pain. But it weighs on me. Heavier and heavier, tearing at the light inside.

My mind spins, but I force my feet onward. The stones grow larger, darker in color. There's a path to my right and a sharp cliff straight ahead. It would take a great amount of effort and some risk, but I could skip the path to climb the hard way. And I would if I knew for sure the spell book was at the top of the mountain. It may not be.

I pause for only a moment to consider before turning to take the long way around. Anxiety crawls over my skin, unsure I made the right choice. But if there is one thing I've learned about the Schorchedlands, it's that it wants you to follow a specific path. If you deviate, you pay the price.

There is a right way. Sometimes, it's the obvious and easy way. Sometimes, it's unexpected.

I follow the path laid out for me and push my doubt back once again.

The air grows cooler and cooler as our altitude rises.

A murmur of voices begin seeping through the stone.

Have you come to complete your mission, slave of the great darkness? the hushed voice whispers over my skin like the wind.

Do you do his bidding? Or your own?

I shiver. Some of the voices are low, some kind, some sinister. I ignore them and continue up the slope, calves burning.

You belong to him.

You are *him.*

"No." The word rushes from my lips between breaths.

"What?" Darren asks.

"Not talking to you," I spit.

"Then who—oh." He floats along with ease, spending no effort whatsoever. It irks the hell out of me that I'm killing myself—maybe literally—to complete this task and it's nothing to him. He just continues with no care in the world.

Raw anger bubbles in my belly.

He's manipulating you.

He convinced you to abandon your mate.

No, I think. *I did that.* I know it was my choice. The wraith was willing to follow me wherever I went, and he was surprised it wasn't to Rev.

He was pleased.

I curl my lip in annoyance. Despite the chill working its way through my clothes and sending shivers over my body, sweat drips down my back.

This is his fault. He did this to you.

Black rage presses over my mind, causing throbs of pain over my brain.

"Tell me what they're saying, child. Say the words aloud if you must. Overcome them."

"They say... they say you're manipulating me. They say you're the real villain."

I swallow, my pace slowing, but I don't dare stop. I don't know if I could begin anew if I were to halt my movement.

If I stop, I really have abandoned Rev. And that is one thing I will never do.

"And do you believe that?"

"No," I whisper.

The pressure over my mind releases in an instant. It wasn't mine, I realize—the rage.

"What else?" he prompts.

Your mate is suffering. Did you know? Would you like to feel his pain?

Breath leaves my lungs, and I stumble. *Keep going*, I chant to myself. *Keep going*.

You are bad for him, always have been.

It's better if you die.

"That Rev is suffering. And it's my fault."

The wraith doesn't immediately respond. "You didn't tell me why you made that choice."

"The spell book. It's my leverage."

"Ahh. Do you intend to trade it?"

My lungs burn. My skin burns as the smoke grows thicker, so do the voices. So heavy it's hard to make out any of them. All for the better.

"I don't know," I admit, teeth clenched, feet still pounding over the loose rubble. I almost slip as the gravel rolls under my feet. Keep moving. Keep going. "I only know," I stop to pant, lungs burning for oxygen, "that the Night Bringer wanted me to chase after Rev. I'm tired of following his plan."

"Follow what you believe, Caelynn." That's his advice. "You are strong. You are smart. You are capable. If anyone could win this chess game, it's you."

My chest tightens because I don't know that I believe him. I've made so many mistakes. I'm stubborn. I'm narrow-minded. I feel so foolish much of the time.

I just don't care what people think. I don't even care what I think, not anymore.

I've always believed what they said about me—murderer, betrayer, villain—it's just... there wasn't another option. I did what I had to.

I am bad. I am dark and foolish and stubborn and

heartless. But I am those things for a reason. I am those things to serve a purpose.

To save him.

And that is what I will do now. I will continue to fight for Rev with every breath in my lungs.

38
REV

The echo of pounding feet, desperate breaths, and spinning confusion washes over me. Have they come back for me?

"Reahgan?" I whisper. It couldn't be him. *He doesn't have feet,* my hazy mind reminds me.

Ow, I think, even though I don't feel much pain. I'm just... heavy. Tired. There is the dull and distant pain of acid on my skin. Of poison in my lungs.

I pant suddenly like I'm running for my life.

My mind is hazy, hardly able to think through where I am and what's happened.

Keep going. Keep going.

My eyebrows pull down in confusion. Who is that? I force my heavy eyes open. Everything is black. I'm still lying on the ground near the tree that once held me pris- oner. *Could I run now?* I wonder.

The harsh smell of sulfur bombards my nose. But I am still in the dark place that should only smell of mildew and blood.

I was in the Night Terror's clutches. Still am, actually. Her sinister darkness surrounds me like a wall, cutting me off from the outside world. Cutting me off from my mate, who's out there somewhere.

Alive.

Where are you, Caelynn?

Gentle dark tendrils curl around me as I lie on the cold ground, body newly healed with no energy left. It's hard to even breathe.

I shiver as the shadow sprites cover me in their protective power. My eyelids flutter.

No, not the shadow sprites. It's her. Her shadows, her essence, are with me, covering me as I lie on the ground, body heavy with resounding pain.

"What is your mate telling you, child?" I wince as the Night Terror's low voice rumbles through the darkness. Coils of the tree's roots slither closer. "Is she almost here?" she asks sweetly.

My mate? She thinks Caelynn is telling me something?

"I've been waiting for her."

I shiver.

The image of a steep, sloping path flickers to my mind, small boots pounding over the gravel. A wraith drifting along.

I swallow. A chill washes over the area, and the branches slithering toward me pause.

Was that Caelynn? She was running up...

The ground rumbles beneath me. "Clever girl. Finally learning something, is she?"

My stomach sinks. "She went for the spell book." Reahgan had told me she left me behind. She continued on.

Quick as lightning, one of the roots shoots up and grips me by the throat, lifting me into the air. I claw at the tree choking me, stealing my breath.

"She thinks she can gain the upper hand. Well, perhaps I've underestimated her after all. It's time to change tactics."

39
CAELYNN

The voices of ancient powers long absent from the land of the living bombard me. Soon, their words are like physical blows. Their breath harsh and commanding.

I push past them, forcing my way through the remnant of their magic.

You are nothing.

You are worthless.

You will fail.

"I am nothing," I repeat. "I am worthless." I agree. "But I will not fail."

"Fight, my Caelynn," my wraith says, his voice full of pride, his eyes full of sincerity. "You are worthy. You are powerful. You are the strongest fae I've ever encountered—and I've met many."

Strong and stubborn and stupid. Yes, that is who I am at the very bones of my soul.

"Your life has been so hard, and you think that your stumbles mean you are weak, but it is quite the opposite.

You have pushed through every obstacle. Even the most evil of monsters could not dull your brilliance."

The mountain rumbles, stones bouncing with their laughter. Is the mountain itself laughing?

"The Night Terror has learned where you are," Darren whispers.

"Good." I am determined, and no spirit alive or dead, evil or good, will stop me.

I pick up speed, letting my wraith's words fuel me. Letting my love for Rev push me further. Using my righteous anger over all the Night Bringer and Terror have done to me as support.

I may never undo it. I may never free myself from their clutches. I may never heal my broken soul or my broken nation.

But I will continue the fight I began when I was an adolescent. If I get the chance, I will kill them.

You cannot have me, I tell the Night Bringer inside my heart.

My magic purrs deep down, dimmer than before but still there. *Believe what you like, child. You are mine for the taking.*

I growl, running harder, faster, through the smoke and raging anger of the spirits on this mountain.

Undeserving.

Weak.

Pathetic.

Nothing.

Evil, just like us.

My boots skid as I pull myself to a sudden stop.

I am three-quarters of the way up the mountain now,

but before me is a fork in the path. One path goes up with an arch of thorns curling over it. One goes down with an arch of shinning black stone carved over it.

I look out past the mountain trails and to the expansive view. Dark lands stretch out so far it's hard to even fathom. The ring of burning red flame glows only a mile away, and beyond it, the green vines covered in thorns that surround the rest of the lands. I can just make out the lands beyond, scattered shades of green. Hazy and vague but there.

Far but visible.

This way, the voices tell me. Streaks of black and red and yellow light soar past me and through the path on the left, through the thorn arch, leading farther up the mountain.

I swallow, panting. A choice. I have to make a choice.

A gentle nudge pushes me right. A harsh rush of magic pushes me left. Well, isn't this a fun game?

"Which way do I go?" I mutter aloud, more to myself than anything, but my wraith murmurs in confusion.

"A riddle, perhaps?" He wafts beside me. "What are the voices telling you?"

"You don't hear them?" I finally ask. I hadn't thought much of it, mostly because I refused to think much of anything. I knew my feet had to continue, and anything else was a distraction. Now... I have to stop. I am forced to consider many things.

"What I hear is for me. What you hear is for you."

"What do you hear?"

He sighs. "Oh, a myriad of things. Some of these spirits I have known personally. They hate me for the choices I made. They are jealous I've been free for many years, working for the temporary Shadow Court Queen."

Temporary. "The Queen of The Whisperwood," I whisper.

"Is not Corranda," he says. Telling me what I already knew but refused to consider. "She is a steward. Holding it only until you arrive to take your rightful place."

I pull in a long breath.

"You, Caelynn, are Queen of the Whisperwood."

I close my eyes, grief hitting me hard. Agony of what I've lost bombards me. I haven't let any of it settle in my mind. What should have been. Those beautiful lands I adored so much, the shadow sprites, the phantoms, my people living in doubt and poverty.

What belonged to me, stolen.

I shake my head. It was lost long ago. I cannot uncover it now. It's too late.

"I'm sorry," I whisper to Darren. To the people thousands of miles away that will never know what I've done. To the shadow sprites.

"It was never your fault, child."

I close my eyes and release a long breath. All of the guilt I've held— I could allow it to swallow me whole. I ache with it, and I accept that ache. But I will not let what I've lost define me.

I have so much good still here.

I may never see the sea again. Or the star scattered sky. But Rev is here, waiting for me. His beautiful silver eyes are worth every star in the sky.

And I also have the admiration of my ancestor. I may

never take my rightful place, but he believes I am worthy of it. And for now, that will have to be enough.

After one long, deep breath, I recall a conversation I'd almost forgotten in all that's happened since. The spirit of the gates. The keeper of the curse.

Keep on the right path.

Maybe she meant what I'd initially assumed, that I should be careful and choose correctly. Or maybe it was a hint.

I examine both paths again. One has thorns which seems correct, in an obvious kind of way. The streaks of magic are obviously leading me that way, but something in my gut says they are not my allies.

I turn instead to the right archway, smooth black stone with geometric sharp edges leading me lower down the mountain. I step closer to the archway and smooth whispers make themselves known through the archway. I can't make out any of the words, but they sound just like the shadow sprites.

Dainty, high pithed, and kind. Not at all like the urgency and harshness of those behind me.

Convinced, I leap through the archway and bound down the path without even considering looking back. Darren squeals, rushing to catch up with me.

I smile. Finally, he's at least a little flustered.

Less than five hundred feet down the hill, the pathway ends abruptly. I skid to a stop, staring out at the drop-off. Then, I turn to a gaping hole in the side of the mountain.

Steam streams from the hole, billowing up in white clouds. I swallow and step inside.

40
REV

I can feel the heartbeat of the ancient beast we call the Night Terror. The very ground beneath my cheek pulses with it.

Boom-boom. Boom-boom. Boom-boom. Picking up speed with every second.

Her voice remains smooth, but I can feel it—she's terrified.

A bitter laugh bubbles up in my chest, and the vines grip my neck again. "What is it you'd like to say, my slave."

"I may be your captive, but I am not a slave. I will never do as you wish."

Her grip tightens over my windpipes, and I wretch. My vision blinks black, the breath is gone from my lungs. She crushes me then drops me back on the ground in a heap.

I cough in as much oxygen as I can manage and press my forehead to the ground. "Let's test that theory. What do you say, child?"

"What?" I cough out between desperate breaths.

Somewhere in the darkness the Night Terror slithers. What does she look like? I still don't know.

"You are going to go to the mountain and reach the book before she does. Or I'll kill her, torture her, while you watch."

A laugh breaks from my lungs. "You don't think I'd really do that, do you?"

"I will destroy you both!" she screams.

I should be terrified. I should be shaking in my boots—and certainly my body is uncomfortable, my heart pained. But I am at ease, deep in my soul.

"Yes, I know that," I whisper. "I believe you."

"Then, you would do as I bid."

"No."

She pauses, slithering closer. Is she examining me? Hot breath warms my neck, sending a shiver down my back. I ignore my own racing heartbeat. My muscles clench and relax.

I ignore the instincts that tell me to run. To hide. To cower before this beast's power.

She has me. She'll kill me. She'll torture me.

But there is only one thing I have control of—my own actions.

"You're going to torture us and kill us no matter what we do. I won't give you what you want on top of it all."

The hot breath recedes. The beast slithers in the darkness. "You wish for a bargain."

Well, no. I hadn't planned for anything remotely close to that. I'd just planned to lose on my terms instead of hers. Like Caelynn told me—we can at least make sure they don't win in the process.

We're doomed, but the least we can do is return the favor.

"*Kill him,*" a voice hisses through the darkness.

"Why?" the Night Terror spits. "We need him."

"*He is the key to her soul. Kill him, and she will fall.*"

My breaths are deafening in the silence. She doesn't speak. Doesn't respond. Chilling realization hits me.

My mind flashes to Caelynn. Her beauty. Her bravery, her strength. Her boldness and wisdom and sadness. She's spent her whole life fighting for mine. She's been so determined to sacrifice herself for me. What will happen if I'm gone?

What will happen to her heart and soul, barely hanging on, if I'm not there to convince her to keep fighting?

My breath comes out trembling.

I'm going to die, but I'm not afraid of that. I'm afraid that my death will cause Caelynn's soul to fail. And the Night Bringer will get what he's been hunting for the last decade.

41
CAELYNN

The steam burns my skin, and I cry out but keep pushing forward. This is the right way, I'm sure of it.

You think you are so clever, don't you child?

I ignore the hissing voice inside my mind. I'd know his voice anywhere.

I've dreamt of it every day since I was young.

A few more steps and the burning steam clears, revealing a perfectly sculpted round room with purple lights flickering on the ceiling. In the center of the room is a platform holding a large, leather-bound book.

I did it. That's my first thought. I found the damn spell book. The book that would save the world from the plague. The book that the Night Bringer so desperately wants.

Eyes pinned to the thick, black leather, I approach the book with careful footsteps. Will there be one last test? One more trial to complete?

I pause, fingers just inches from gripping the powerful pages in my hands.

"What's wrong?"

My eyes flash to the wraith, Darren. I had forgotten he was even here.

"Take it," he instructs, his voice full of awe.

Should I? I know the Night Bringer and Terror want me to have the book. They want me to use it to free them. Doubt flits through my mind.

Maybe I calculated incorrectly. Maybe they manipulated me again. That wouldn't be so surprising.

We will kill him.

I pull in a breath.

One finger on that book and your mate's heart will stop.

I pull in breaths through clenched teeth.

"Tell me," Darren says softly. He knows I'm hearing more.

"This Night Bringer," my voice breaths. "He says they'll kill Rev if I take the book."

"Doesn't a threat show you are doing the right thing?"

"The right thing for who?" I whisper.

I try not to let my fear take over, to let my grief show, but I know I fail. I know because of the way Darren looks at me.

Pity and fear. Pain and sadness.

The wraith looks over his shoulder, through the steam where the exit lies. "Caelynn, my child," the wraith whispers, black eyes meeting mine. "Perhaps I was wrong."

My eyebrows pull down. "What do you mean?"

"The Shadow Court will never know what you've done. Just as they never knew what I did. For them. For the world. But this—this is your destiny, child."

My lips part. "What?"

"I have never been more sure of something my whole life. Our people may never be what they once were, and I will mourn that with every remaining moment of my being, but I feel it. This place. You. Me. Our people will be responsible for saving it all. And that is something I can forever be proud of."

I blink rapidly. "What—what are you saying?"

"Take the book, Caelynn," he whispers.

"What?" I gasp. "But what about Rev? You... you want him to die."

"No." His voice is sure, sharp. His face tilted down in determination.

"You promised." My voice breaks.

"I will not go back on my promise to you, child, but the book is your destiny. It calls to you. Don't you feel it?"

Black streaks of magic ripple from the leather binding. *Caelynn*, the whisper pours from between the pages.

"Take the book, and I will do the rest."

"But—"

"I love you, my daughter. I am sorry for this bitter fate of ours. It is terrible. But it is beautiful. As are you."

The wraith wisps through the wafting steam, and when I blink, he's gone entirely, leaving me alone with the spell book whispering my name.

42
REV

I struggle for breath, limbs twitching, but I don't bother fighting the branches crushing my windpipes. I can feel her power, even though I can't see her.

Night Terror.

My life seeps away slowly. She's savoring it—my death. I won't ever know what she is, what she looks like.

Is this what Caelynn endured before my brother's death? She was only seventeen when that happened. This is what she killed my brother to avoid.

I'll never see her golden eyes again, I think as the claws of death reach into my soul like a fluttering bird. Gentle, peaceful, dark.

Death is here to take me home.

Are you ready, child? The voice is smooth. Patient. Caring.

It's not at all how I expected death to come.

Especially after my experience with the Black Gates. The anger I'd felt then is nowhere near me now. I have no regrets. No questions. *If only I'd known.*

And thank God I learned the truth before it was too late.

I know who my mate is, and I don't hate her. I adore her.

I'd burn the world down for her. My lips curl into a small smile as my body convulses one final time, extremities growing cold.

"What the hell are you smiling about," she growls, branches gripping tighter, but I don't feel it anymore. My mind is elsewhere, my body entirely numb.

I am at peace with my end. I only pray Caelynn will join me in the afterlife.

"We had a deal!" someone yells. "You said you wouldn't hurt him!"

Something slams into my back, my mind fuzzy. The warmth I'd felt rushes out, leaving bitter cold and muscles contorting in agony.

Glowing red power streaks from the ground in the form of a massive hand. It clenches over a wraith, struggling in its grip. I blink back the brightness, even though I know it's dull.

"Please," Reahgan begs.

Reahgan writhes in the translucent hand of magic. I cough, air rushing back into my lungs roughly. I blink and try to adjust my sight as quickly as possible. This may be my only chance to get a sense of my surroundings. I'd been in complete darkness before.

Where is she? Where is the Night Terror?

The red glow brightens the area. I can see the uneven tree trunk streaked with black scars, a few clawing branches, but no other forms. Where did she go?

"I promised not to kill him. And I didn't." The ground trembling along with her words, making it impossible to tell where the voice is coming from. How do I fight something I can't see? "I never claimed how long that offer would last. He's been alive for several hours. Surely you didn't think the deal was indefinite—that I'd *never* end him?" She chuckles, and I shiver.

"Run, Rev." Reahgan's voice barely escapes him. I blink, my mind still hazy, but I remember who he once was. Young and handsome with sharp jawlines, pale skin, and dark hair. He was poised and confident. Powerful.

I can't picture that fae in this wraith now—laid powerless and pathetically writhing, his face distorted in pain and grief.

I shift, measuring what my muscles are capable of.

Roots shoot from the dirt and wrap themselves around my wrists before I even begin. "Not so fast, little fae."

The red magic tosses Reahgan's wraith form to the dirt at my feet.

"Please," he begs again, face contorted in agony. "Please, spare him. I'll do anything."

He'd do anything to save me? I shake my head from my confusion because it doesn't matter.

"You had the chance to do what I wanted, and you failed. And now, you will watch your brother die."

I don't know which one of us she's talking to. I suppose it doesn't matter.

"Emotions are worthless, child. You'd have done well to have learned that lesson long ago. They make you weak."

"Like your love for the Night Bringer?" My brother's voice is harsh, angry.

"Yes, exactly like that. Do you think I'd be here if it weren't for him? No. No, I'd be free to manipulate the living right alongside him. But I'd foolishly chosen love."

My eyebrows pull down.

"That was my first curse. A human trait I'd fallen into."

"You don't love your mate?" I whisper through my aching throat.

"Of course not. I've learned to rid myself of that curse long ago."

"Yet you will bend the world to reunite with him?"

"I will break the world to reunite with him. But not for sentimental reasons. We are one, child. Two parts to a single whole. That is all. We will reign, together. Because together is how our power will reach its fullest. He needs me to free himself from his own stone prison. I need her to free myself from my cursed prison. It is a simple matter."

My breaths are still heavy, my windpipe and chest burning with the effort it's taken just to remain alive.

"You, however," she hums, her voice drifting closer, "have benefited from the love of your mate." Her words wrap around me like a caress. "But it has only delayed your final death."

I wince, preparing for the blow I know is coming. The roots tighten on my wrists, but there is a flash of something dark in the glowing red light, and a stone drops into my palm.

Warmth spreads over my body like the glow of my magic—except I haven't done it. I open my palm, and sure enough, my Lumistone glows softly.

What the hell? I'd lost it in my fight with Reahgan and the manticore. How...

"You," the ground rumbles. I force myself to stand on wobbly feet.

"Hello there, dear old friend," Caelynn's wraith murmurs, his smoke form dancing over me, as if— protecting me? Why would he... unless Caelynn is...

My heart sinks. "Where is Caelynn?"

"She has the spell book."

The tree growls, anger shivering even the stone below my feet.

"And we'd like to make a deal."

43
CAELYNN

Take me. Use me. Bend me to your will.

The whispers rush from the book, its magic wafting from it in waves of cold and warmth. Power pulses, eager for me to wield it. A red glow emanates from deeper in the cave, and behind me a cloud of white steam blocks sight of my exit.

My fingers ache to grip the leather binding, to feel the power.

Yesss.

I stumble a step back, realization and panic hitting me like a truck—it reminds me so much of the Night Bringer's magic. Will I be able to control it, or will it take control of me?

I am not like the Night Bringer, the book hisses softly.

I wrinkle my nose. "Well of course you'd say that."

"Come closer, shadow fae."

I jump at the voice, so much louder now. Closer, even though I've stepped two feet back.

"I will show you," it says.

My teeth chatter, still unsure. But I came all the way for *this*. I can't wimp out now. If this book is as evil as the Night Bringer and his mate, then I am doomed either way. At least this way, the chances that the Night Bringer will take my soul and get what he wants are slimmer.

"I have every answer you've ever sought. I can show you all or nothing, you choose. You can wield my knowledge, no one else."

Me. "No one else?" I knew the Night Bringer needed me to use the book to break the curse. But am I the only one able to use the book entirely?

"Only you as of three days ago."

"What happened three days ago?"

"Your father died. I don't suspect you'll want to know the details."

Dead.

Icy cold grief whooshes through my already weak body. I haven't seen my father in a decade. I hadn't expected to ever see him again. And yet—it hurts to know he's gone.

Since the wraith brought up the Night Bringer going after my father, that's been stuck in my mind. I technically knew he had the right blood but not the power needed, and so I hadn't thought more of it. But if the Night Bringer grew desperate—

"How?" I force out of trembling lips.

"The Night Bringer persued him, though he fled to another court. When cornered, your father took his own life."

I press my hand over my mouth. Another life stolen by

the Night Bringer. I don't even want to get into how in the world a book would know about it.

"I am the Book of All, shadow fae," the book whispers. "I know all."

I look up to the pedestal, soft purple lights twinkling above it. "You know all?"

"All that has been, yes."

"But not the future?"

"No. That would be impossible, and rather impractical, seeing as it changes moment by moment."

I force myself up on wobbly feet. "Okay, book, tell me this." I feel so utterly stupid talking to a book and calling it by name, but I will admit it's a decent distraction. "Where is Rev?"

"Your mate is with the Night Terror in the valley below the mountain."

My knees buckle, and I barely catch myself.

"Is he alive?" I barely force out of my broken lungs.

"Yes, though he's had a few close calls these last several hours."

I swallow. "I need to save him. How do I save him?"

"That is not how it works, shadow fae."

I shake my head. "I need to know!"

"Ask another question."

"Where is Darren?"

"Darren is currently making a bargain with the Night Terror."

My eyes widen. "A bargain?" I breathe.

"An exchange, to be precise. The spell book for your mate's life."

This time my knees do buckle, and I slide back to the ground. "Is that wise?"

"That is not the kind of information I hold, shadow fae. I can only tell you what is, not what should be."

I nod quickly, waving it off. "It was a rhetorical question."

"I see."

"What are you?" If the power I'd worked so hard for was information, I'd take all the information I could get.

"An ancient spirit. I was once a powerful being, not unlike the keeper or the Night Bringer and his mate."

I shiver. "You told me you *weren't* like him."

"I said I was *once* like him, and I only mean as a species, not in character. What you are does not define you. Your actions define you. Your choices."

That doesn't make me feel any better.

"I am bound to the book, and though his power has been limited, he is free with a living body and power he can use of his own fruition. I have none of those things."

I shake my head, unable to wrap my mind around all of this. "Show me," I tell the book, taking the offer he'd mentioned moments ago. I need to know if I'm being manipulated, and this is the only way I can think of to get closer to understanding.

"You simply must touch my binding, and I will show you but an ounce of what I know so as not to break your fragile mind."

I groan. *Wonderful.*

Still, I stand back up and step toward the damn talking book. I allow my fingers to gently rest on the thick leather, and immediately, I am transported.

I am blasted with colors, my body soaring through time and place. Images flash through my mind of massive beings walking on the earth. Mountains rising and falling. These beings crush the stone like a pebble beneath their feet.

One being glows bright red, one lapis lazuli, another violet. All glow brightly with power so intense I can't comprehend it.

"The creator gave these creatures dominion over a land separate from the earth." The book's voice echoes through my mind. "And each gave their power to their portion of land. This created the elemental courts as you know them. Adolescent fae take power from the very nature around them. That magic lingers forever and ever, for all time, even once the beings of power have passed. Our wars wiped many of us out. Conflicts with beings from other worlds have banished others. My sister and I volunteered our souls to be cursed to stop others like us who would otherwise have used their power to reign unjustly over the fae we created."

"Your sister?"

The image of an emerald being as tall as the mountain with thorns sticking out of her limbs flickers into view. "The Wicked Gates."

"Indeed."

Next to the emerald being is a red being burning with fire. "Flicker Court," I whisper.

"I gave the fire magic to the land that is now the Flicker Court, yes. Many of our kind gave their power to the land and then buried themselves in the ground, happy with their completion. My sister and I remained, hidden in our lands, longer than many others. When the Night Terrors rose to power, we were one of the last able to resist them."

Inky black tendrils dig into the earth like a massive worm, and I flinch away from the sight.

"They had become corrupted by the promise of power. They enjoyed pain. They sought to destroy, instead of create. And so, with the help of some of the of fae rulers of the time, we managed to banish one of them to the Schorchedlands. It took many sacrifices. Every curse must have a reversal. I condemned my own soul to protect the book with the power to reverse the Night Terror's curse. My sister sacrificed her soul to protect the borders around the cursed lands."

And that worked for centuries.

"Yes, the Night Bringer has been trying to break these walls for five hundred years."

"So, I suppose you aren't exactly happy to see me."

"If I had laid dormant for all of time, my purpose would have been fulfilled, yes. But I placed my soul inside because I did not expect it to be so easy. So, I am not surprised to see you, shadow fae. I know much about you, as you can imagine."

I laugh awkwardly. I suppose he would, wouldn't he?

"You are strong but vulnerable. You may yet lose the fight for your soul. But I am not disappointed in who stands before me."

I bite my lip. "What do I do now?"

"That is up to you. You are the last being with the power to obtain my knowledge and use my power."

After another moment of thought, I am confident in what I have seen. It could be mind-shattering, certainly. I could delve so deep into the history of our world and the worlds beyond this one, but—at least right now—I don't much care about the origins of our world. I care about now. I care about Rev. He is alive. And this book is the only leverage I have.

"Is there any way to kill them? The Night Terror and Night Bringer?"

"Is it possible? Yes. Can you, Caelynn of the Shadow Court or your mate achieve this alone? No."

Wonderful. "You say alone. How about with your power?"

"The majority of my power is in knowledge. I can give you spells to use against them, but without more raw power, no, it will not be enough."

"So, we can't win?"

"You cannot currently win in a fight against the Night Terror."

I suppose my wraith has the right idea then. Bargain our way out. The problem is, how do we bargain with them without setting the evilest of beings to ever walk this realm free?

44
REV

Roots break free of the ground, shattering the world and sending chunks of ashen dirt pouring down on me. I cover my head and then scramble to move out of the way.

I rush forward, through the darkness, unsure where I'm even going.

"This way, princeling."

I follow the wraith's rushed voice and claw my way up a mud-caked slope.

"She won't kill you yet. She wants to hear the bargain first, but you shouldn't linger all the same."

I follow a subtle stream of dull light to the surface. The mountain comes into view quickly, black smoke rising into the sky. Behind me, that massive tree half the size of the mountain trembles, it's claw-like bare branches vibrating and then... growing.

What the hell?

I flee from the crumbling stone and the dirt ground cracking and caving in. The tree—the tree is rising.

Roots the size of the manticore's chest fly from the dirt and slam into the ground. The trunk twists and groans and then rises on the exposed roots like spider legs.

I fall to the ground, mouth open wide as the most hideous of beasts is revealed. Two red eyes blink, and a mouth with three rows of sharp slimy teeth sit just below it.

I can't take my eyes off of the horrible sight.

The tree—the Night Terror, I now realize—shivers, shaking off the rest of the lingering soot from its spider-like legs. "Now…"

My breath trembles at the sound of her quaking voice.

"Tell me this bargain before I end your pesky existence once and for all."

The wraith chuckles, crossing his rippling smoke arms. "The princeling for the spell book."

"That sounds like a fair bargain." The tree rumbles, it's teeth dripping with saliva.

"This prince, of course." He places a hand on my shoulder, and it sends a blast of cold through me.

The Night Terror laughs. Her red eyes grow and then narrow. "And here I thought you meant the wraith prince."

"You and I both know only living-beings can be a prince."

"I wasn't quite sure." The tree shifts, three of its roots —legs—scuttling forward, shifting her closer, lower. "In that case, I do not see the point in such a bargain. What would I do with the book? It's been within my reach for five hundred years. I do not need the book. I need the being able to *use* the book. I had wondered if perhaps she was willing to trade her soul for her lovers? Hmm? Now, that is a bargain I could agree to."

"No!" both the wraith and I yell at the same time.

"We will not give you her soul," the wraith continues more smoothly.

"Then, I would be better off crushing the princeling's body to wound her soul even deeper. She is on the verge of failing, you know. So close."

"I am surprised you'd botched that pathetically, to be honest. To allow the prince to send a piece of his soul to heal her? My, my." He tsks and shakes his head.

A piece of my soul? What does that mean?

"They have not been mated. I did not think..." The ground trembles as she growls. "It does not matter. The oversight will not happen again."

The wraith pauses, his eyes narrowing. What is he thinking? Did he learn something new just now? I watch his expression as he seems to come to some unpleasant conclusion.

"She has sparked his soul stone. They are as good at mated."

A shimmer of light appears in the wraith's chest but then flickers out. What is he doing?

The Night Terror hums, her legs twitching. My stomach roils. I don't understand so much of this conversation.

"The boy could, in theory, complete the spell. With him alive..."

My mind spins, trying to keep up with what is happening.

"I have twice the options." The Night Terror's legs click

as she bends, bringing her trunk lower to the ground. She's still massive, but her eyes and teeth are closer. "It is an interesting thought. However, it is only useful if is it possible to bend their will to mine without the loss of her soul."

I pull in a breath, my mind going dizzy. She can't take Caelynn's soul. It's mine.

The ancient being's red eyes shift to me. "Would you complete the spell to save yourself, child?"

My mouth falls open. *What?*

Rancid breath tosses my hair back, and I nearly gag on my boots.

"Bring her to me, and we can discuss this bargain."

Slithering black roots shoot from the earth and grab me by the neck. I scream, clawing at the ground as I'm dragged back into the rotten soil.

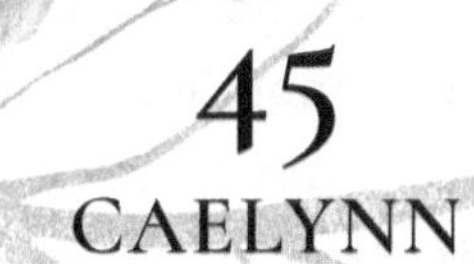

45
CAELYNN

I recoil, pain ricocheting through my chest like a knife just carved its way through me. *Rev.*

How—*how do I know it was Rev?* Hell if I know. But I do, deep down.

"What just happened to Rev?" I bark at the book.

"The Night Terror retook him. He is not seriously harmed."

I take what little comfort in that as I can. *Keep moving,* I chant to myself. *One step at a time. I can still save him.* I grip the book in both hands, lifting it from the platform.

A pounding of magic booms as it breaks free.

"What the hell was that?"

"The release of power. Nothing to be concerned about."

I swallow, holding the massive tome to my chest. I can't believe I'm conversing with a book.

"You'll want to hurry. The Night Terror is not terribly patient, and she enjoys killing."

"It'll take me an hour to climb down the mountain."

"Not if you shadow walk."

"But that'll use up too much of my magic. I'm going to need it, aren't I?"

"Unlikely. With me, you will have an extra boost in power. And to be perfectly honest, no matter how much magic you hold, you cannot fight your way out of the Night Terror's clutches. Your strengths right now are speed, determination, knowledge, and possibly stealth. So, unless you intend to leave your mate behind, it should not be a significant deterrent to use your magic now."

"Permission to shadow-walk. Got it."

———

I take my book friend's suggestion and begin a very quick descent down the mountain by leaping from one path level to another. This process only takes about fifteen minutes until I find the flat trail heading toward the valley where I know the Night Terror to be.

I scan the valley but pause when I notice something strange—the massive tree east of the mountain is gone. "Where did that massive tree go?"

"The Night Terror has relocated closer to the mountain edge. You will find her if you continue on the current path."

I frown. That's not exactly what I asked...

"Yes, it is."

I shake my head, uninterested in arguing with a damn book.

I sprint east, around the bend at the bottom of the mountain pass, and finally, the claw-like branches of the massive tree come into view. How did a whole damn tree move? Next to it, stands the massive figure of the manticore with his obsidian horns, red eyes.

"She walked," the book says matter-of-factly.

Only a moment later, more figures come into focus. The manticore holds a body, limp and swinging by its ankle. Beside them, two wraiths float with jerky movements.

I bite the inside of my mouth as I realize the hanging body is Rev.

But I won't show them my pain. My terror. My doubt.

I will fight until my last breath, which I am certain will be moments from now.

You can't win, the book had told me. I can't defeat the Night Terror, but I have some things on my side.

"Put him down," I croak, my voice so much weaker than I'd planned on.

The tree rumbles with laughter. *That voice.* It sends black waves of panic over my body. I feel his claws digging into my chest. His black magic creeping inside of me.

The tree is the Night Terror. Her mouth is a gaping hole filled with several rows of slick fangs.

I press my eyes closed, clenching the book tighter.

Easy, shadow fae, the book whispers. *The Night Terror cannot touch me. And therefore, cannot touch you so long as you hold onto these pages. Keep me on your person, and you are safe from her.*

I bite my lip. That's why she didn't want me to take the book.

So, the Night Terror cannot touch me while I hold the book. But the manticore can.

My eyes refocus on my most pressing enemy. Kill the manticore, then I can get Rev out of here. If she can't touch me… it would be a matter of maneuvering the right pieces. First step: kill the manticore. Step two: get Rev in my grasp.

Step three: flee.

"That will work, right?" I mutter to the book.

It is possible, yes.

I pull in a breath, recentering my focus. Rev's limp body swings from the manticore's grip. He doesn't move. Is he unconscious?

Save Rev, that's my goal now.

I slide my feet wide, muscles clenched and eyes pinned to my target. "Does a backpack still count?" I ask the book.

That will do just fine, shadow fae.

I swing my backpack from around my shoulder and quickly stow the book inside. Placing the bag snuggly to my back, I clip the front straps.

"You've come bearing gifts, I see?" The Night Terror's voice sends chills down my spine.

You will never be free, my magic whispers. *Either she will kill you or I will.*

I curl my lip, exposing my teeth—pathetic compared to hers. But I don't care. I will kill anyone that comes between me and Rev.

"Put him down," I demand, voice clearer now.

"Very well." The Night Terror's horrific lips curl into a smile that chills me to the core. Then, she nods, and the manticore releases him. Rev falls fifteen feet, and his head smacks the stone, followed by his crumpled body.

I gasp and jerk forward. *Please be okay. Please be okay.*

His body lies in a heap, limbs bent awkwardly. He doesn't stir.

"Do you desire vengeance, little fly?" the manticore says with that low voice. Eerie.

"A useless battle, child," the Night Terror advises. "You are too weak to pick such uneven fights."

Useless? Perhaps. But I long for the chance to win one battle, to take something from the Night Terror before she takes from me. To even the playing field just a little bit.

He is her most important weapon.

"Even if you win and escape, you cannot both pass through these walls," the tree rumbles with a powerful voice that shakes me to my core. No matter how much determination I muster, I cannot stop my body from reacting. "One of you will be trapped here with me. Which will it be?"

I grip my iron dagger in one hand, an obsidian dagger in the other. Rev will leave with the book. I don't know if they can use it to cure the scourge without me—the book did say I was the only one able to use it. But he'll have done his job. It won't be his fault the book failed.

We'll have stopped the real evil, and that's what matters most.

"And that will leave you in my grasp."

"Yes," I whisper. She'll torture me. Kill me, if I'm lucky. But Rev will be free, spell book in hand. And even if the Night Bringer steals my soul and takes control of my body, the spell book will be out of my reach. We'll both be trapped here.

All will be right—or as right as it could be.

My plan solidified, I focus on my target.

I pull my prickly shadows around me, and I leap once, twice, three times, and land on the manticore's shoulder.

He swings at me before I can land my first blow, but I shadow leap to his other shoulder. I am barely larger than his head.

Calling me a fly was not so much of an exaggeration.

He roars in annoyance, his hooved foot crushing the soil just feet from Rev's fallen body. I leap again, landing next to my mate. He stirs, a groan escaping his lips, but he doesn't open his eyes. I ignore him. For now, I have more important issues to deal with.

The spell book's magic rushes forward just as the manticore's foot flies down at me and Rev. With a boom, my blade connects with his scaled hoof, and it slides into the soft spot in the middle. Not far enough. Not a large enough wound. But the beast reels back with a roar of anger and pain.

I leap again before he has the chance to regain his balance and carve my blade into the soft spot under his ear. Holding onto the hilt with both hands, I throw my weight into it and slide down his neck. His massive hand flies and smacks my body away as if I really were a fly. Or perhaps a wasp. I intend to sting.

I land shoulder first on the gravel, sliding onto my back, but the pain doesn't even register. I hop back up without a moment to catch my breath, ready to end this. I am numb to pain. Numb to fear.

He grabs for me, roaring in pain and anger, but he is slow. Black blood now flows freely down his neck to his armored torso. His scaly tail swishes, back and forth.

I leap several times in rapid session—by his feet, clinging to his upper arm, back to Rev. I fling my iron blade through the air and then leap again. He jerks as I land on his shoulder but bounce back in an instant.

My blade finds its mark—his left eye—just as I manifest right before his face. I kick the hilt, slamming it as deep as I can manage. The squishing sound and splatter of gook and blood churns my stomach, but the taste of victory distracts me.

His roar turns to panic as he claws at the blade, carving his own nails into his flesh.

Panting, my feet find solid ground. The manticore's dying groans echo through the valley, and finally, he falls face down, body limp.

I'm not given even a moment to enjoy my victory before five massive roots shoot from the ground and clamp down on Rev's body.

I scream. His dark eyes meet mine just before he's dragged below a cage of tree roots.

"You didn't think it would be that easy, did you?" the Night Terror whispers, her voice riding the acidic wind. Ash begins to fall gently, and my heart falls.

I beat the manticore. She can't touch me so long as I have the spell book.

And it's still nowhere near enough.

I turn to face my enemy, my whole body trembling.

"Hello, my pet." Tremors quake through my body and I close my eyes. I don't know if I can do this.

I could still win. I could walk out of here, and she'll never be able to touch me. If I could find some ounce of hope in a world without Rev, I could do it.

You faced a being just like this one once before.

"And I've never gotten over it."

But you walked away, alive and with the upper hand.

I swallow.

"Well," the Night Terror drawls pleasantly. Seemingly not at all bothered by the loss of her minion. "Now that that business is over and proved fruitless, let us move on, shall we? Now, I have the spell book in my sights. There are many possible bargains to be struck. Who would like to offer first?"

My soul shudders. I could save Rev by giving the Night Terror what she wants. But I would doom the world to their mercy, and I know better than to think we'd be free from their terror. I cannot make that trade.

I'd be better off letting us both die.

Seek the right death. I swallow. The right death. I can die so long as my soul remains alight.

Is there an afterlife? I ask the book.

Yes, the book whispers.

"This is the afterlife, you foolish girl. You've seen it. Walked through it. This is all there is!" the Night Terror roars. "The afterlife is *my dominion.*"

My knees tremble, but I keep my body upright, my shoulders straight. "I wasn't asking you."

Yes, child, the book whispers. *There is more. Not all will see it. But there is light on the other side of the darkness.*

"Caelynn has made her choice," the Night Terror calls out. Darren blinks at me. I'm unsure what the expression means. Is he displeased? Shocked? Had he expected me to condemn the world to save Rev? I would, I think. Under the right circumstance. But I've bargained with these beings before, and I will not do it again.

There is no victory here.

"The princeling doesn't seem in the right frame of mind to respond just yet." One of her many crooked legs nudges Rev's limp body.

I wince. His eyes flutter open and find mine again.

"I forget how fragile living beings can be."

I clench my teeth tightly. I swear one of those beady red eyes winks at me.

"Let us move on to the wraith."

Darren flinches. "What?"

"I can give you exactly what you desire," she purrs, pressing closer to my ancestor's spirit. "I will bargain it away to you in exchange for your help gaining what I desire."

"What I want is Caelynn free of this place." His voice is low in annoyance.

"You desire a powerful ruler of the Shadow Court. I can give you that."

He curls his lip, baring sharp black teeth that are a fraction of the size of hers.

"I can see inside your head, don't you remember? You've admitted so many times that you would do things differently if given the chance. You wouldn't have sacrificed your court to trap me. Isn't that right?"

"The Night Bringer ruling in her place is not the same."

"Isn't it, though?" The Night Terror's voice rises. Her trunk twists and groans. "I can make you promises. If you help me destroy her soul, my mate will take her body—"

My hand flies to my mouth. I stumble back, feeling the Night Bringer wriggling inside of me. His acidic black magic crawling, burning.

No. no. no.

The Night Bringer is crawling through my veins, his magic slithering, waiting, seeking the right moment to suffocate me from the inside out.

"My mate will promise to make the Shadow Court what it once was. It will not be destroyed by our domain. And with her body, I will ensure she continues the Shadowspell bloodline. It is a good deal."

Darren's eyes flicker to me, pain and guilt so fucking obvious that black rims my vision immediately. *He's considering it.*

He promised, but we never sealed it with magic.

I remember my dream. He told me what would happen. He told me the Night Bringer would rule the Shadow Court in my body. And he's going to let it happen.

I squeeze my hands into tight fists.

"You will promise never to harm my lineage and allow them to rule in peace."

"We will."

"No!" I roar, anger suffocating me.

Rev stirs, groaning and twisting on the ground. My relief is short-lived.

"Kill him," the Night Terror instructs my wraith. "She cares for you. Her anger is already pushing her closer to the edge. If you were to kill her mate—here, now, before her— she'll fall into our grasp."

The Night Bringer's claws rack at my soul, dark talons carving deeper, sending my mind into a void of darkness. My eyes fill with tears as he pushes harder. I claw at my chest, digging my nails into my skin. I can't reach him.

I can't stop it.

He's trying to pull me under.

"Caelynn," Rev croaks, so close.

I fall to my knees beside his prison. His hand reaches out from between the branches holding him. I blink but turn my attention to my betrayer.

"If he dies by your hand," the Night Terror continues, eyes pinned to Darren, "I will consider our bargain complete. Act. Now."

I stand between my mate and my ancestor, chest heaving, lips trembling.

For a moment, only a moment, the wraith hesitates. Then, horror warps his expression, and he leaps at me, claws flying, teeth bared.

Rev screams.

I barely know what's happening when in the next instant, I am on my knees, sharp pressure on my back. Agony explodes in my chest, warmth spreading slowly.

My eyes drift down to my torso where a clawed wraith hand, inky grey smoke wafting and sizzling, has plunged out from my chest.

"I'm doing this for him," a voice so much like Rev's, and yet not at all, whispers in my ear. "It's what he wanted but was too cowardly to take. He will thank me when it's all over."

My heart sinks, breaking all over again.

Crimson blood with streaks of black pour from the wound, and I crumple to the harsh ground.

Death would be a mercy, another voice tells me.

46
REV

One moment Caelynn is standing over me, facing my would-be attacker with fierce protective-ness. The next, my brother is on her. He carves into her back with clawed fingers.

Something inside of me shatters as she falls to the ground face first. The warmth in my pocket burns like fire but flickers with ice-cold emptiness.

Through tear-streaked eyes, I watch Reahgan pull his hand from Caelynn's chest, his smoking hand dripping in blood.

Caelynn's wraith friend leaps at him, roaring in rage. "No!" he screams.

I grip my prison of branches with both hands burning hot with magic I can't control. White-hot power blasts my cage open, and the Night Terror hisses but then rumbles with laughter. "It's too late, boy."

I scramble to Caelynn's side and violently flip her limp body over. I can't feel anything but the panic now. My head and heart pulse together, roaring booms through my mind.

How had all of this happened? I don't remember much. The manticore grabbed me, squeezed my neck until I'd passed out. And the next thing I knew, Caelynn was fighting him, her sure movements, sharp eyes, and magic rippling off of her in waves.

I don't know how she got here or what kind of deal she may have made for my life.

What I do know is that her wound is pouring blood, her face is slack, and her eyes are entirely black.

"Caelynn," I whisper before yelling, begging. "Caelynn!"

She can't be dead. She can't die now.

She doesn't respond. She doesn't move.

Behind me the wraiths battle. The manticore's body lies between us.

With shaking fingers, I gently brush the fabric of her shirt away from the gushing wound. The skin is greyed, the blood as black as her magic. My magic is low, but my palm flickers, eager to save her. I hesitate, wondering if it's wise.

Should I let her go? If I heal her body, will the Night Bringer take her? Will I just be wasting my magic?

"Kill her," a pained voice mutters. "She must die. Completely." Caelynn's wraith.

The hair on my arms stands up straight as an iron dagger skids over the rocky ground and bounces off my knee. Steam lifts gently to the sky where the two wraiths had been fighting, and I know at that moment that Reahgan is gone. I can't bring myself to even care.

He loved me. And if I ever get the opportunity, I'll mourn for him. But today, right now, it's her I care about.

Through teary eyes, I look up to Caelynn's wraith. My

eyes narrow at the strange expression on his face and the soft glow of golden light emanating from his chest. "I thought you wanted her alive and me dead."

The wraith looks up into the hazy red sky. "He'll take her if you don't do it."

Caelynn's body convulses in my arms, her mouth opening in a silent scream.

"It's already begun," the Night Terror says. But she doesn't move. She doesn't come for us.

"Caelynn!"

"Do it now! Destroy her body so he cannot take it," the wraith cries. "She'll die thinking I was willing to betray her," he adds in a whisper. "But it must be done."

"No." I whimper. I can't do it. How could I...

"*You are weak.*" The voice coming through Caelynn's lovely lips is gravelly and sinister. Not her.

The breath freezes in my lungs.

No.

"*She is mine now.*" Caelynn's lips curl into a cruel smile.

"No!"

Panic and desperation take over, and my magic flares to life again. I blast my healing magic into her body, violent and harsh. Her whole body convulses, mouth foaming, and then she falls still. Her wound has stopped bleeding, but otherwise, I'm not sure what good I've actually done.

Her eyes fly open, and they are glowing golden, almost auburn.

"Caelynn!" I call, elation flooding me. It worked!

"Kill me," she croaks. "Please." Her face crumples, and black tears streak across her cheeks.

The dagger is in my hand. An iron-studded, obsidian

blade. So much like the one that killed my brother—that began this whole terrible journey.

I press the blade to her chest with trembling fingers. Her soft flesh sags against the blade. I should obey her wishes. This time... this time, it's the only thing that makes sense.

The Night Bringer has her, he's stolen her soul and will take her body. He's already begun.

"*You cannot have her,*" I say through clenched teeth.

"Death would be a mercy," her voice hisses, her eyes black. I can't tell who's talking. Her, or the monster inside.

Her pupil glows red. He's there. He's taken her. She laughs manically. "*You are too late.*"

I failed her, I realize. This happened because her soul disintegrated. Because she didn't love herself enough. If I was better for her— if I had tried harder to show her what I now see...

It was my job as her mate to save her.

"You promised you wouldn't leave me." I heave with sobs.

She is not gone yet, princeling. This voice is soft, and... inside my mind? *Feel your soul stone. It still warms. Her soul remains yet alive.*

"Who are you?" I whisper through my tears, but those stranger's words echo through my mind, sparking hope. A tiny light in the darkness.

And I feel it. The warmth pulsing in my pocket. Gripping the little stone between two fingers I pull it out. It's my Lumistone, the one I plucked just before the High Court ball. It feels like a lifetime ago. It's just a little berry turned to stone with time but... it's glowing.

My eyes widen. The wraith gasps.

You have the power to heal what no other can. You have the power to undo their curses.

"You are going to save her," the wraith whispers.

Caelynn convulses beneath my hands, back arching. She gurgles black liquid and forces out cruel laughter.

The smoke magic that makes up my mate's wraith lightens, and a golden light flickers in his chest, growing brighter. "Tell her," he whispers. "Tell her she saved me."

I don't have time to ask what he means. Or wonder why the golden light has taken over his being. His smoke magic dissipates and flutters away in the wind.

This time, when I use my healing magic on Caelynn, I do so with confidence. I delve into the mystery that this is my fated mate. Terrifying and lovely and everything I could have ever hoped for in a soulmate.

My hand glows bright white, and I press it as far into her wound as I can. Eyes closed, I feel her. Her dark essence, enigma and stealth, beauty and passion and determination. So much bravery. And kindness. And protectiveness.

When my mind loses all time and place, I don't recoil. I press deeper into it. Into her. It's a void, vast and empty. Abandoned.

No, I whisper in response to that feeling. *I won't ever leave you, Cae.*

Raging winds begin to blow. *Leave,* the Night Bringer demands. *You are in my domain now.*

But I ignore the voice because he is wrong. She is here. I can feel her.

Weak and dwindling but still pulsing with the tiniest of warmth.

A small ember glows in a pile of cooled coal.

My mate, I whisper.

The ember flickers but fades again. I take in a long deep breath just as the storm begins in earnest. A tsunami of shadows roar toward me, but all I see is her.

My white light brightens the void and streams directly into the dying soul of Caelynn, my lovely shadow fae.

47
CAELYNN

Every nightmare I've ever had is nothing compared to the agony I feel now as my life slips and he takes me. The Night Bringer's jagged talon carves its way through me, splitting my very soul.

This time, I know I am right that the Night Bringer has taken my soul. Everything I am and was and will be. He has it in his very hands, and he will crush it.

All I know is pain.

It is who I am. Who I will be.

I am drowning, suffocating, burning alive, and being flayed all at once. And it doesn't stop. It continues on and on, for all of eternity.

I will not leave you, Cae.

The pain halts for only an instant. Then, it comes crashing back into me. The controlling rage slams down on my weak heart.

A rushing wave is coming, I can feel it. Harsh hands grab me, hold me, caress me. Hands that I do not want to let me go. I take hold of his magic, unsure how but willing to take it.

My lifeline.

48
REV

Caelynn heaves in a desperate breath and claws at my arms. I hold her, press her to my chest.

"Caelynn?" I barely dare to hope.

"Rev," she cries.

It's her; she's awake. She's here.

Terrifying hope fills me, and I hold her close.

"What happened?" she asks as her nails claw into my skin. I don't even care. This pain is more than worth it.

I hold my Lumistone tightly in my palm. It burns bright and true. My mate is here, with me. Home. "I don't know."

Neither my brother nor her wraith are anywhere to be seen. It's just us, lying in the valley below the mountain.

Then, the ground beneath me booms, and a massive shadow looms over us.

"Do you suppose this means you've won?" her voice trembles with rage. The Night Terror's red eyes blink down at us. We are but flies to her. Pesky rodents she requires.

Pets. Slaves.

I swallow.

"He will take her back. And even if you think she can keep control of her soul now that you've saved her, what now?" she whispers, amusement clear in her tone. Her finger-like branches twist and turn like stiff snakes. Her roots scurry like spider legs, causing a near-constant tremor in the ground.

I look over my shoulder. We are miles from the Wicked Gates. Caelynn weighs heavily in my arms, her body limp. She couldn't walk herself out of here, not with her injury, and who knows what kind of mental state she's in right now.

The Night Terror is right, I don't know how close she'll be to succumbing to that darkness inside of her. It's not gone. It's just under her control—for now.

"All I have to do is crush your skull, and she will falter once again." Her fang-filled mouth twists into a smile. "And you have to escape me and all of my friends."

I shiver as the groans begin. Distant at first, but they grow quickly.

I pull Caelynn into my lap, cradling her. Her eyes are lidded, barely open, but I can feel her fire, her muscles relaxed. I hold her tightly, realizing that I'd saved her from that fate only temporarily.

Crooked, grey limbs appear over the bank of the swamp, and several bodies pull themselves out of the water. They crawl, unable to walk. But I watch in horror as dead bodies pile out. Hundreds of them. Thousands.

My mouth falls wide.

Then, wraiths appear, whipping through the flame wall and floating toward us. Soon, the army becomes so thick it blocks out what little light of the sun we can still see.

A wall of obedient wraiths has come to the Night Terror's beckoning and have created a shadow so thick it may as well be night.

"Do you see the hopelessness now, princeling?"

I wince, keeping my eyes closed. The knife weighs heavy in my hands.

We're both going to die.

And, well, dying is the better of the two possibilities for her.

"Unless," the Night Terror purrs, "you'd like to make a bargain with me."

My breath comes out ragged, trembling. Caelynn stirs against me and wraps her arm around my neck. She pulls herself up so her lips are at my ear, her fingers gripping me tightly, desperately.

"No," she whimpers but says no more.

"No," I echo, and she relaxes against me once more.

"You haven't even heard the deal."

"Why would you make a deal? You have us where you want us, don't you?"

"I am confident in our ability to win this war once and for all. But I wouldn't mind... speeding up the process." Her eyes flicker to the blade in my hand.

I could end it now, I realize. That's what she's afraid of. If I carve Caelynn's heart out now, her hope would be lost. We would both die. But they would lose.

That is what Caelynn wants.

"If you were brave enough, perhaps you could sabotage us just before your death," the Night Terror admits. "But there is another option."

Brave enough. Am I brave enough to kill her? Am I strong enough to take her life like I'd promised so long ago? Now that I know who she is. Now that she is mine.

"Use the spell book," the Night Terror says with a smooth voice. Tempting. Taunting. "She has it in her bag."

My eyes flash to a bag hanging off of her shoulder. She has it? She reached it?

"Break the curse. Free us."

My mouth falls open, eyes wide, stomach twisting. "Wh-what?"

"Open it. Use your soul stone..."

I open my palm to stare at the flickering gold and black light inside the Lumistone. Is this what she means? "I thought... I thought only Caelynn had the power to break the curse?"

"Yessss," the Night Terror hisses. She crouches down, lowering herself. "But your mate connection allows you certain... abilities. You can use enough of her magic to unlock the spell book and use its power."

I blink. And release the Night Terror from her prison.

That's what Caelynn's wraith was talking about.

"You heard the bargain I offered the foolish wraith, yes? I am generous. Free us, and you can have all you desire."

I frown.

"I will allow you a happy life with your mate. A long life. With children, if you wish. No more running. No more fear."

My stomach twists, hope flutters in my chest again.

It couldn't be that easy...

"Name your terms, princeling. Consider what you could gain."

I don't dare look her in the eyes, but I do consider. If I were to complete a magical bargain, they couldn't touch us. Ever. "

"You would be bound if I freed you—," I mutter, unsure if I'm talking hypothetically or... not. "You and your mate would never touch Caelynn or me ever again. You'd never order anyone to attack us. You'd never hurt us, directly or indirectly. And the same promise will hold for any children either of us may have."

"Yessss." She shivers eagerly, but my head is screaming not to do it. My heart is screaming to do anything to save her.

What will they do if freed? How many will die because of their terror? How many more lives shattered?

I look down at my lovely shadow fae. No one has ever chosen her.

Tears stream down my cheeks at all she's endured. The loneliness. The grief. The guilt. She believes herself worth-less. It's why her soul has faltered so deeply.

This is how it will end.

The Night Bringer has been free for five hundred years. The world hasn't ended. What will he do once reunited with his mate?

I stare at the dagger still gripped tightly in my fist.

My choice is to doom the world to save myself and my mate.

Or kill her myself.

I would have to shove this dagger into her heart, here

and now. If I don't—they'll win anyway. They'll take what they want with nothing to stop them, with no bargains or deals to restrict their rule. I can't keep Caelynn's soul alive indefinitely.

Kill my mate or free the villain who terrorized us for the last decade.

"Your choice, princeling."

I pull Caelynn from my chest and look down at her peaceful face, eyelids fluttering. She moans softly. For the second time, I hold the dagger tip to her chest, right at the red dot I'd created the last time. Her skin buckles. A tiny prickle of blood pools at my dagger point.

All of it—every ounce of grief and pain and fear—it all comes down to this.

It cannot end this way. This can't be all there is.

A terrible desire stirs up in my belly. Dark ambition. Will I kill another to save her as she did me?

Could I make the same choice she did?

Am I as strong as Caelynn? Stronger? Am I even capable of the kind of selflessness this would take? I know what I have to do. What I must do, no matter the cost.

My muscles clench, arms pressing harder, chest heaving in sobs.

The ground rumbles with bitter laughter.

Choose.

49
CAELYNN

Light and peace are all I know for moments at most. He holds me, comforts me. Loves me.

And then, the pain is back. Pressure on my chest, sharp talons carving into my heart.

Night Bringer.

No, not this time. This is him.

Rev.

He's... going to kill me. My mind spins. He'll end it. It hurts. My heart aches that I'll never know what it's like to love him completely. I'll never know what true happiness tastes like. The game is over. I always knew I wouldn't win. I could only ensure the enemy fails. And that's what he'll do now.

I am ready to die.

Agony takes over, my mind flickers black.

The ground shakes, building until it's a full earthquake. Shattering. Crumbling.

Laughter. My monster is laughing. His mate joins him.

Their laugh becomes one, soaring like a symphony of suffering and rage. Bitter. Pained. Terrible.

Power is sucked from my body in that one quick moment, and my thoughts are wiped silent. My mind quiets, and finally... there is peace.

50
REV

The army of wraiths scatter to the winds as the mountains fall, the ground splits, cracks, opening to the void. The fire wall tips over, sending roaring flames over the miles surrounding it, scorching the land with streaks of black scars, and thick smoke rises to the sky.

I remain there on my knees in the valley surrounded by death. I stare at her peaceful expression. Eyes closed, mind spinning over what I've done as the world around me implodes. I allow it all to take place without moving an inch.

An hour must pass before I dare to look up.

When I finally do, I am alone. The Night Terror is gone. The bodies she'd raised have fallen limp where they stood. I'll have to climb over them to get out of here. But now, it seems, the path is quiet.

My hands gently cocoon Caelynn's head, cradling her limp body in my arms, and begin the long journey from this place.

I won't leave her here. I couldn't leave her here.
She is mine. And I will not fail her again.

51
CAELYNN

Gentle rocking sets my body at ease, even as my mind spins. My body is numb. Slowly, a tingle begins in my fingers. It crawls up my arms and to my chest, which buzzes with an uncomfortable prickling.

I force my dry eyes open, and I see the sky.

Midnight blue, almost black, and scattered with stars glowing gloriously. Their patterns distract me, but I can't focus on any one constellation. It's beautiful. I just wish I could stay still to get a better look. But my head sways, making the twinkling stars continue to move.

I wasn't supposed to ever see the stars again.

I groan and try to pull my head up.

"Shh. We're almost home."

Home?

Confusion and hazy memories twist over my mind. A dull ache grows in my limbs. "Rev?"

"I'm here," he tells me.

"What... what's happening?" I whisper. Where is he taking me? What is home? I haven't had a true home in over a decade. Does he mean the cottage? Does that mean we are still alive?

My veins run cold. No. We couldn't be alive. Is this home something else? Have we somehow passed beyond? To the light the spell book told me lies beyond the darkness.

"Heaven?" I mutter, words failing me.

Rev's chest rumbles with laughter. "Not yet, angel."

I groan and cling to his neck. Rev is carrying me, I realize. I am cradled in his arms like a child. I curl into his chest, willing to take the moment of happiness—even though I have no idea what's happening.

Are we okay? Are we running from the Night Terror?

Rev doesn't seem to be in much of a hurry. I blink as the stars are hidden behind translucent white leaves, shining rays of light all around. "Where..."

I watch the leaves peacefully drifting by. Maybe I don't want to know. Maybe I just want to feel this peace. This warmth. Contentment I haven't felt in... well, ever.

Minutes pass, and the leaves disappear, exposing the star-scattered sky once again.

There's a rustling and the mumbling of voices, but I twist into him, face hidden in his neck. He holds me tightly. "We need to rest. Tell my mother of my arrival when she wakes."

My breaths become more labored as he carries me into the building and up the steps. Then, he lays me on the softest bed I've ever felt in my whole life.

I gasp as his arms release me, taking his warmth with him. But then, all at once, he's back, his chest and legs against me. His arm curls around my waist, and all I can think is, *this is perfect*, just before I fall asleep.

52
REV

I jerk when the door slams open.

Rusty dagger in hand, I blink rapidly. My mother stands in the doorway, her hand over her mouth.

"You're home," she breathes. Her eyes flicker to Caelynn lying peacefully beside me.

"Yes," I whisper.

She frowns as Caelynn stirs, then groans, her expression crumpled in confusion and discomfort. My muscles are stiff and aching, my limbs weak. I can only imagine what she's feeling now.

"Rev?"

"Shh," I tell her and brush the hair from her face.

Her eyes crack open, then her sight flashes to my mother in the doorway and she jerks up, holding the covers over her chest like she's hiding something intimate. She's fully dressed in the ragged clothing she entered the Schorchedlands in. Or perhaps she's hiding the tiny prick where I'd almost stabbed her.

Caelynn sits, panting, expression covered in confusion.

"Mother," I say. "Will you call in a maid? Caelynn could use a bath."

"She…" My mother's mouth gapes open. I have to remember that Caelynn is not an ally or friend or anything else to my mother. She's an enemy.

She's the assassin that murdered my brother in the room across the hall.

Heaving in a long breath, I pull myself out of bed. "Wait here," I tell Caelynn. "I'll send someone to draw you a bath in a moment."

Caelynn frowns and doesn't respond. I suppose it is a lot for her to take in.

"I don't understand," she mutters.

I lean over her. "I promised I wouldn't leave you there."

Her eyes widen then dart past me to my mother still watching us slack-jawed. I have a lot to explain. To everyone.

"I'll be back in a few minutes," I tell her and then head out into the hall to speak with my shocked-silent mother.

She stumbles back into the bright hall, and I shut the door behind us.

"That's…"

"Caelynn. Yes," I say, rubbing the back of my neck.

"You… she…" My mother is a lovely, eloquent woman usually. Poised and calm. Good with words. Not so much today. Her eyes flicker dark, the bright silver flashing. Her dark hair is braided down her back.

"She is my mate, mother."

What little color was left on her face drains entirely. "No," she breathes.

"It's taken me a while to come to grips with it too."

She shakes her head rapidly. "No. Even if it's true. Even if…"

"She saved me," I say simply. The story is so much more complicated than that. She's saved me time and time again. I've only just returned the favor. I still owe her everything.

"I—that… that doesn't matter. Mate-ship doesn't matter." Her cheeks turn blood red. "You do not have to choose her, Reveln. You…"

"I know that," I say.

I pull my flustered mother into my arms, holding her tightly. I don't expect her to understand. Not now. Not so quickly.

"But I do anyway."

She knew Caelynn and I had worked together in the trials. She knew Caelynn was helping me with my quest after, and though she wasn't particularly pleased, she'd never commented on it. That was my father's job.

But now, things are different.

I don't know how things will change. I don't know what it means between us. But Caelynn is my mate. And I will fight for her.

53
REV

When I walk back into my room, Caelynn's big eyes meet mine. I pause, taking it the sight.

She's still a wreck—her hair disheveled, muck covering her body, bruises line her arms and bags are under her eyes.

But she's here. Safe.

Home. In my bed.

"Rev." Her voice is hoarse. Her eyebrows furrow. "What the hell happened?" she whispers.

I slowly approach the bed and sit beside her. She doesn't meet my eye now.

"A lot," I say. Because I'm not sure how to explain it. How to even find the words.

"I'm so confused."

I take in a long breath. "I told you I wouldn't leave you there."

Her lips part. "But... at what cost?"

I swallow. Only time will tell. I ignore her question because I can't bear to dwell on that now. She's here. We're both safe and alive and free. What happens in our world now that those monsters are free—well that's a problem for tomorrow.

"We're home and safe. Let's focus on that, okay?"

She shakes her head, still staring at the soiled sheets. Blood and dirt streak across the once shiny material. "Why?" she whispers. "I'm not worth it."

I suck in a long breath. "In that, Caelynn, I can promise, you are wrong."

A gentle knock sounds on the door. "The bath is prepared, Prince Reveln." The squeaky voice comes through the door.

"Thank you," I call. "Come on, let's get you cleaned up and we can talk through some more of this over a decent meal."

Caelynn blinks rapidly and then nods. She scoots out of bed slowly and walks around to meet me. Her eyes are distant like she's only half here with me. "Are you okay?"

She shivers but nods. She glances out the window. "What happened to the wraiths?"

"Most of them were set free, I think."

She meets my eye. "Where is Darren, then?"

"Who?"

"My wraith... my..."

"Oh," I mutter. "He... I'm not sure exactly what happened but I don't think he's—with us anymore." I'm not entirely certain he died, it was more like he ceased to be.

She grimaces.

"He... did he help us? It's all such a blur." She runs her fingers through her hair.

"He did. And he told me to tell you, that you saved him. I don't know what that means but…"

Her lips part. "Did he die?"

I shrug. "He began to glow and then disintegrated into dust, I think. I assume it was some kind of spell by the Night Terror."

A short laugh escapes her lips. "No," she says. "He was redeemed."

54
CAELYNN

My mind is slow to move, stuck on small matters, unable to force my way to the biggest issues.

All I keep thinking is that I'm here, in the luminescent court palace, as a guest. I'm currently sitting in a porcelain tub filled with warm, pleasant-smelling water, in a massive bathroom with glistening white tiles. The sun, bright and cheery, streams through the skylights in the ceiling.

I don't think about the details, about why it's a ludicrous notion, for me to be here at all. I only know that it's strange.

Like a dream.

I sink deeper in the tub, the water a dark brown from my disgusting state. It will take three or more baths to rid myself of the grime of that place. Maybe it will be with me forever.

I think about Darren. My wraith ancestor is gone.

I think it's good that he's gone. He healed his soul. He...

overcame his biggest weakness by choosing to help me instead of further his own desires.

He was a wraith. And somehow, he loved me like a daughter.

I'll miss him. Another strange notion.

Part of me wonders if I died, and this is the afterlife. Because none of this can be real.

Except, it's also hard for me to imagine that my afterlife could be this pleasant.

After a very long while, someone knocks gently on the door. When I don't respond, the door swings open slowly. Rev peeps his head through the crack.

"Everything okay?" he asks.

"Fine," I mutter. I sink a little deeper into the mucky water, hiding. I'm not sure why I'm hiding. But this—this isn't our relationship. Rev and I.

Is it?

I suppose I'll have time to figure all of that out too. Time. Another luxury I have a hard time wrapping my mind around.

"I don't mean to rush you but... we have visitors."

My eyebrows pull down. "Visitors?" I know my mind isn't working at full capacity right now but—who would ever visit me?

"The High Queen just arrived on property. She's—going to have some questions for both of us."

SHADOW OF THORNS

To the world, Rev is a hero. To those who know better-- he's doomed the fae realm to destruction.

Rev succeeded in the most important mission of his life: he came home with the spell book that can save the realm from a terrible plague.

Except, in order to save his mate, he used that book to destroy fae hell and free all of the beings inside. Including an ancient and evil being with a plan to rule over the fae realm. He doesn't know when or how, but the Night Bringer will be back, now at full power.

So between parades in his honor, and the queen declaring him the new High Heir, Prince Reveln must secretly work with the convicted shadow fae the rest of the fae realm continues to hate, to stop the Night Terror before it's too late.

AUTHOR NOTE

Thank you so much for spending your time reading my books and getting to know these characters. It means so much! This series was both wonderful and stressful to write (we were smack in the middle of a pandemic at the time!) but it's also so fulfilling.

This series has been a blast to write and there's so much more to come for these characters! The final two books are available now!

If you'd like to keep up with my writing, get behind the scenes intel and maybe even get your hands on additional stories from this world, please join my newsletter.
You can find the sign up form on my website:

www.StaceyTrombley.com

I'd also love it if you'd leave a review for my books! Reviews make a huge difference for authors and to be honest I just want to hear your thoughts!

And lastly—I'd love to hear from you. Be my friend! Instagram or Tiktok @StaceyTrombleyAuthor

ABOUT THE AUTHOR

Stacey Trombley is a casino employee by night, urban fantasy author by day. She lives in Ohio with her husband, son, and German Shepherd, Riley. When she's not writing or reading, her husband is probably dragging her along on one of his crazy adventures for his travel vlog or competing against him about who can pick the most Survivor winners in the first episode (hint: she's winning). But mostly, she's probably reading.

www.ingramcontent.com/pod-product-compliance
Lightning Source LLC
Chambersburg PA
CBHW031146160726
47991CB00004B/1574

9798988748106